The
Orphan
and the
Mouse

by Martha Freeman
drawings by
David McPhail

Holiday House / New York

HOLIDAY HOUSE is registered in the U.S. Patent and Trademark Office.
Printed and Bound in April 2015 at Maple Press, York, PA USA.

3 5 7 9 10 8 6 4 2
www.holidayhouse.com

Library of Congress Cataloging-in-Publication Data
Freeman, Martha, 1956–
The orphan and the mouse / by Martha Freeman;
illustrated by David McPhail. — First edition.
pages cm
Summary: In 1949 Philadephia, Mary Mouse and an orphan named Caro embark
on an adventure when they team up to expose criminals and make the Cherry
Street Orphanage a safe haven for mice.
ISBN 978-0-8234-3167-0 (hardcover : alk. paper)
[1. Mice—Fiction. 2. Orphans—Fiction. 3. Orphanages—Fiction.
4. Human-animal relationships—Fiction. 5. Criminals—Fiction.]
I. McPhail, David, 1940- illustrator. II. Title.
PZ7.F87496Or 2014
[Fic]—dc23
2013045488

ISBN 978-0-8234-3451-0 (paperback)

For every teacher and librarian who reads aloud
to children, in particular Jean Anderson,
my second grade teacher,
who read us *Stuart Little*.

Chapter One

————⬥————

Crouched in the shadow of the door, Gallico watched the mouse approach. It was a full-grown male, no doubt a member of the colony that lived inside the walls.

Usually the mice stayed well out of Gallico's way. In fact, he had a hard time distinguishing one from another. Still, he knew a few things about them. They regularly raided the pantry and the dining room for crumbs. They maintained a system of portals between their territory and his own. On school days, two or three liked to hide themselves in a classroom and listen to stories told by the teacher called Miss Ragone.

Gallico found human stories boring. Unlike the mice, he was not a deep thinker. But in the end, where did all that thinking get them? In the end, who had the claws?

On this particular night, Gallico had found himself locked out of the boss's apartment on the third floor. It was winter, chilly even indoors, and he had come downstairs to see if he could insinuate himself into the soft bed of someone with warm feet. The most likely candidate was the human kitten called Bert, who slept in the boys' intermediate dormitory. Gallico had been on his way to see if the dormitory door might be open when his nose and whiskers detected the presence of a mouse in the boss's office, and, bloodlust quickening, he went to investigate.

Gallico loved the taste of mouse—the sharp bones, pebbly teeth, chewy tail and all. It reminded him of when he was a kitten on the street, a time when fresh mouse was the most luscious delicacy he could hope to enjoy. In those days, there were never enough mice either for him or the tough crew he ran with. As often as not, he went hungry.

Gallico's fortunes changed when his looks attracted the attention of the boss, Mrs. Helen George, headmistress of the Cherry Street Home for Children. A pretty cat would add a cozy touch to her apartment, she thought. As a bonus, his natural instincts would dispatch any rodent trouble that might arise.

Gallico was lured indoors by a fish head in a saucer. After that, he never left.

Like most cats, Gallico was adept at personal grooming and adept at killing. Thus his responsibilities to the household aligned with his skills, which were also his pleasures. A vain cat leading a life of ease, he grew self-indulgent and self-satisfied without ever losing his taste for blood.

Now, as the cat watched, the mouse made his way toward the nearest portal, which meant he was moving in the cat's direction. This was strange. Strange, too, was the confident way it moved. As it came near, Gallico saw that it had squares of paper clutched in its jaws. Ah, yes. Now the cat remembered something else about the mice in the walls. Periodically, one of them would climb the boss's desk and steal a few of the paper squares she kept there.

Why they wanted to do such a thing, Gallico didn't know and didn't care.

By this time the cat's nose was quivering, his tail twitching. Still, he held himself in check, prolonging the delightful anticipation of the game to come. With its irritating nonchalance, this mouse had earned more than the usual torment. Gallico would squeeze every last drop of pleasure from the doomed creature's final moments.

At last, when the mouse was three lengths of a cat's tail distant, it turned its head and...looked squarely into the hot yellow eyes of its fate.

Chapter Two

Zelinsky Mouse did not stop to wonder what had gone wrong with the Predator Warning System. He'd always believed it was fail-safe, but apparently not. With no time to spare, he dropped the pictures he'd been carrying, changed direction, and ran all out for the backup portal in the corridor.

The predator was bloodthirsty and cruel like every one of his kind, but he was also well fed, old, and slow. Zelinsky thought he could outrun him . . . and indeed achieved his goal before he felt the first brush of a claw.

He was safe!

Except . . . what was this? His nose hit solid wood, a barrier. The portal had been blocked!

Zelinsky died of a broken neck. There is no need to dwell on the crass details of what he endured before. Better to consider the sweet poignancy of his final thoughts for his loving mate and pups, the last meal they had shared, how they had laughed and squeaked and touched noses, not suspecting their goodbyes would be forever.

"Skitter safe, Papa," said Margaret, his most anxious pup.

"Your papa always does," said Mary, his mate.

Millie and Matilda both asked him to come home with a story.

In his mind's eye, Zelinsky saw each beloved face clearly. He might have had faults, but he knew he'd been a good family mouse.

And after that, he knew no more.

Chapter Three

❖

Every morning Jimmy Levine awoke before the other boys in the intermediate dormitory, put on his robe and slippers, then padded down the hall past the kitchen and dining room, through the foyer, out the front entrance, and down five steps to the walk. There he retrieved Mrs. George's copy of the *Philadelphia Inquirer,* which he carried into her office and laid on her desk.

Even though it meant getting up early, the job was coveted as a mark of Mrs. George's favor. The child who brought in the morning paper had to be both reliable and trustworthy—this last because he was allowed in Mrs. George's office alone. No other child, or adult, for that matter, ever went there in her absence.

Ten-year-old Jimmy had earned the job in the fall, and by this particular winter morning knew his way so well that he didn't bother turning on the lights. Thus it was pure chance when, leaving the office, he looked down and saw a tiny square of paper protruding from beneath the rug.

Ordinarily not a scrap was out of place, so Jimmy knelt to see what this could be and saw…a green three-cent postage stamp with an illustration of a man and a cart. *Minnesota Territorial Centennial 1849–1949,* it read, *Red River Ox Cart.*

The stamp was kind of interesting, Jimmy thought, like a

tiny window to a faraway place and time. Jimmy guessed the Red River must be in Minnesota, and a hundred years ago pioneers must have used carts like this for hauling. An ox was like an oversized cow, it looked like. They didn't use carts in Minnesota anymore, did they? Trucks and trains more likely, same as everywhere else.

Thinking he'd look up the Red River in Miss Ragone's atlas, Jimmy went to put the stamp on Mrs. George's desk.

Then he had a thought.

Mrs. George would know he was the one who put it there. No one else could have. What if she asked him about it? What if she thought he'd been messing around with her stuff?

Jimmy didn't trust Mrs. George. One time she'd accused him of eavesdropping, lost her temper, and boxed his ears. Later, when she realized her mistake, she gave him the plum job of bringing in her paper, but she never apologized.

Now Jimmy hesitated. Keeping the stamp was out of the question. He was no thief, and anyway he had no one to send a letter to.

What if he put the stamp someplace Mrs. George wouldn't notice right away—like, uh...inside the little box with the pattern of white triangles on the lid?

Jimmy opened the lid, noticed the single, old-fashioned gray metal key inside, laid the stamp beside it, closed the lid, and replaced the box exactly where it had been before.

With any luck, it would be a good long while before anybody found that stamp.

Chapter Four

Bad things are forever happening to mice, which is why the well-run colony has in place an MMRP (Missing-Mouse Response Plan). Thus, Zelinsky was barely an hour overdue when scouts were dispatched to look for traces and, if necessary, perform the grim duty of retrieval. Soon after that, spy network staffing levels were doubled to increase monitoring of human conversations. Any mention of *mice*, or worse, *exterminator*, would be reported immediately to the chief director.

Shortly after dawn, the scouts returned to report they'd seen no sign of Zelinsky. What they did bring back were the pictures he had stolen, four of them found scattered on the rug of the boss's office.

"Only four?" Chief Director Randolph asked the squad leader.

"Only four," the squad leader replied with more confidence than he felt. Having heard the footsteps of a human pup, his squad had rushed through their final sweep. He hoped they hadn't missed anything.

"So be it," said Randolph, who then confiscated the pictures, saying they were necessary to the investigation, when in fact, he, the squad leader, and every other Cherry Street mouse knew they would find their way into his personal collection.

Two weeks passed, and the spy network reported no mention either of mice or of exterminators among their human neighbors. Randolph ordered resumption of normal staffing levels. Every mouse breathed easier.

At this same time, Zelinsky's bereft family hosted a memorial ceremony attended by all the colony's luminaries, including the chief director himself. As was traditional, a modest feast was offered and heartwarming stories were told. From them emerged a portrait of Zelinsky as solid citizen, loving father, and unlikely art thief.

Any pup could tell you an art thief had to be brazen, bold, and daring. The epitome was Zelinsky's immediate predecessor, Andrew, who had been nothing short of a legend. Zelinsky was brave, certainly, but also staid and conventional. In fact, shortly before Zelinsky's death, these qualities of his prompted a quarrel between him and his mate, Mary.

What led up to the quarrel was this.

A week before Zelinsky disappeared, a delegation of disgruntled mice had come to him with a formal request that he challenge Randolph for the chief directorship.

Randolph by this time had been in power for nine generations. His principal interest, critics said, was no longer the good of the colony but rather the good of Randolph. Just look at the number of pictures he had appropriated for himself.

The size of his personal collection was an affront to every right-thinking mouse.

New blood was needed!

And who better for the job than Zelinsky? He was young, big-eared, and energetic. He had a high-visibility job. He was honest.

Mary had been exhilarated by the prospect. She would advise her mate, and she was full of ideas for colony improvements: Galleries should be established to make the art collection available to all; additional story auditors should be trained and deployed in the nurseries; the long-stalled Sentry Communications System for Colony Defense (SCSCD) should be completed and deployed at last.

And that was just the beginning. Together, she and Zelinsky would lead the colony boldly into the future!

Or not.

Because when Mary had shared this vision with her mate, he had wiped his whiskers with exasperating thoroughness and said, "Why would I want the headaches? Our family has a clean, cozy nest and a growing collection of pictures. Let some other fellow challenge Randolph. For myself, I am comfortable with my life as is."

Mary had reasoned, squeaked, and pleaded . . . to no avail. In her frustration, she had called her mate "dull as daisy stems," which hurt his feelings. Later she apologized; they touched noses, made up, and agreed no one would ever know of their quarrel.

Zelinsky disappeared the following day. He had not yet declined to stand for chief director. Only he and Mary knew that that had been his intention.

Time passed; spring came. In May the Cherry Street directorate made an unexpected proposal. Would Mary Mouse care to serve as art thief?

Every mouse knew that the directors had been having a hard time finding a new thief, but none had seen Mary's appointment coming. True, her father and grandfather had both held the post, and she was known to be agile and quick thinking. Still, the idea of a female art thief took some getting used to. This was 1949, and even among mice, ideas about appropriate gender roles were more rigid than they would later become.

Mary hesitated before accepting. Her pups had recently lost their father. Wasn't this too great a risk? But when she called a family conference, the girls told her to take the job.

"Art's important, Mama. The colony always wants more. You would be a great thief, and so you should do it," Millie said.

"Besides," said Matilda, "it'll be neat having our mama be art thief. The other pups will envy us."

"Hush, Matilda." Margaret shoved her litter mate with her tail. "That's not what matters, is it, Mama?"

"What matters to me is the three of you," said Mary. "But to be honest, I want to serve the colony. Also, a new challenge might help me get over losing your papa."

"Then you have to do it," the pups agreed. And so it was

decided. Mary Mouse became the eleventh art thief in colony history. Soon some mice were saying she was a better thief than her mate had been—if not, of course, up to Andrew's standard.

By midsummer, Mary's position was secure. What's more, the contingent of mice who had sought out her husband began to speak of Mary as a candidate for chief director.

No delegation had yet approached her, but Randolph had heard the rumors. Thus the Cherry Street colony was ripe for political upheaval on the Saturday night in August when Mary Mouse set out to learn her new assignment.

Chapter Five

Shortly after dusk, Mary entered the chief director's nest and found him reclining on a divan built to his own specifications from shoebox pieces and sofa stuffing. The divan was impressive for its size, but more so for the number of pictures decorating it. There were two dozen at least, still only a fraction of the chief director's collection.

The Cherry Street colony's fascination with art had begun some thirty generations before, when an ordinary forager called O'Brien happened upon a picture on the dining room floor. It was blue, its subject the head of a full-grown human female.

Little suspecting the sensation it would cause, O'Brien had brought the picture back and—using the glue that conveniently coated the back—affixed it to a wall in his nest. The neighbors came to see, then their neighbors, then mice from every sector. Up till then, no mouse had ever looked so closely at a human face, and soon O'Brien's picture was all any mouse could squeak about.

What was the blue lady looking at? What was she thinking? Why had she arranged the fur on her head that way? What was the significance of the white ruffle around her neck?

Then—inevitably—"Where can we get pictures of our own?"

Responding to the popular will, the directors dispatched scouts who identified the picture's provenance as the plateau atop the boss's desk. When in time it was discovered that new pictures appeared there at intervals, the job of art thief was created.

Even as the mice craved pictures, they knew they dared not be greedy. If they took too many, the boss would investigate, jeopardizing the safety of the entire colony. For this reason, supply never met demand, and mice like Randolph hoarded pictures the same way a miser hoards money.

Now Mary took a moment to admire the variety and color

of the pictures adorning Randolph's divan before raising her whiskers and dipping her snout in deferential greeting. "Chief Director," she said.

"Mary Mouse," he replied. The runt of his litter, Randolph had spent a lifetime compensating with comestibles. Randolph's admirers considered his girth, in particular the fat rolls around his neck, to be visible signs of his outsize position in the colony. Mary, not an admirer, found the fat rolls repulsive, especially this evening, when they were speckled with the remains of the cookie crumbs he'd eaten for breakfast.

"Your assignment is straightforward," he told her. "The spies report a new shipment of art has arrived. Can you go tonight?"

New art was something to celebrate. "That's wonderful," she said. "Yes, of course. Is the Predator Warning System fully operational?"

Randolph blinked. "I've spoken with the monitors myself."

"Thank you," said Mary. "And do you know the nature of the picture?"

"A portrait of a male human, purple, I believe, but that is all the scouts have learned. Can you get five copies?"

"Five copies," Mary repeated. She dipped her snout again, then flipped her tail in farewell. Randolph responded in kind, and Mary was dismissed.

With time before her departure, Mary went to the west sector nursery to retrieve Millie, Margaret, and Matilda. They were her youngest pups and the only ones still in the nest. Now that Zelinsky was gone, they were probably her last litter. For a treat, she took her girls to the central larder. The human cook, Mrs. Spinelli, had made macaroni and cheese the previous night, and the foragers had brought back a generous supply.

"Mama, do we have to go back to the nursery right now?" Millie asked when they were done eating.

"Wipe your whiskers, dear," her mother said. "We have a little while. What would you like to do? Go to the playground?"

"Stories!" the three pups chorused.

Their mother feigned surprise. "Stories? Really? What do you want to hear about?"

"Papa!"

"All right," said Mary. Gathering the three girls close, she wove a tale in which their papa donned white clothing and sailed on a boat in a storm. Neither Mary nor her daughters knew the exact meaning of sailing on a boat, but the auditors had brought back word of this exotic activity from the story of the mouse named Stuart Little, a great hero to the colony. Sailing, every mouse agreed, must be very exciting.

"More stories, Mama!" Matilda begged when Mary was done.

"Not now," Mary said. "Now I must go."

"Scurry safe, Mama, won't you?" said Margaret.

"I'll be back to tell you a story before bedtime."

Because art thefts all proceeded according to protocol,

16

Mary had not needed detailed instructions in order to carry out her mission. Now she left her pups at the nursery, grabbed a dried cricket wing from the larder and munched on it for strength as she followed the main pathway through the foyer, turned left under the stairway, and trotted straight along the west wing corridor.

As she traveled, she was greeted by near and distant relations going about the nightly business of the colony. The first female art thief was something of a celebrity; some mice even moved aside to let her pass. Her better nature told her this was silly. She was just another hardworking mouse—no more important than a builder, a nurse, or a garbage manager.

Still, if she was honest with herself, she had to admit she kind of enjoyed her status. And really—didn't she deserve special treatment? Her job took boldness and skill. Not just any mouse could do it.

There was a border outpost where the west corridor intersected the wall between the boss's office and the girls' dormitory. The guard there was young, brawny, and sure of himself.

"Greetings, Auntie." He dipped his snout.

"Nephew," she greeted him in reply. The two mice did not know exactly how they were related, but all colony mice were family, and *Nephew, Niece, Auntie,* and *Uncle* were the usual appellations.

"No sign of the predator tonight?" Mary asked.

"The monitors report he is confined."

"Very good," said Mary.

"Scurry safe," said the guard, and—with a flip of her tail—Mary left him.

From the outpost to her destination was a short distance, and soon Mary was peering out at an expanse of polished oak flooring, a rise of carpet, and, in the distance, a formidable wooden structure—the boss's desk.

There was nothing in her view to alarm her. The shelter's hushed nighttime sounds were peaceful. Still, Mary hesitated, watching, listening, and sniffing. Then she took a breath for courage, straightened her ears, and nosed her way into human territory.

Chapter Six

Outside the wall, the smells—dust, human skin, the fur of the predator—were as expected. The temperature was cool, the spaciousness dizzying. Alternately dashing and pausing, Mary made her way across the smooth wood, then climbed up onto the rug, its thick pile tickling her belly.

The boss was unpopular among the mice for many reasons, among them her tidiness. With no snacks along the way to distract her, Mary moved swiftly, stopping only to catch her breath at the base of the desk before beginning her ascent.

Owing to powerful paws and lightweight bodies, mice are outstanding climbers, and Mary scaled the desk like a mountaineer, push-pulling her way upward using the tiny, almost invisible crevices in the dark wood. Upon achieving the plateau, she surveyed its landmarks—a leather blotter with cream-colored paper, an address book, a telephone, a fountain pen on a crystal stand, an inkwell, and an ivory-inlaid box in which the boss kept a key.

For Mary, the most important item on the desk was a round brass container approximately her own size. In its side was a slot from which protruded the loose end of a roll of paper. This was the artwork Mary sought.

Recovered from her exertions, full of anticipation, Mary approached the container, tilted her head, and studied the new picture. *Leave it to Randolph to get the color wrong,* Mary thought. *This portrait is more pink than purple.* She would take time to appreciate it later. For now, she noticed only a narrow face, large eyes, a moustache, and a full head of hair. A *sad-looking fellow,* she thought, and wondered whether the picture would be popular. There was no predicting mouse-ly taste. Perhaps sad would be in vogue this year.

Either way, Mary's job was to return the artwork undamaged. So she tugged and gnawed, tugged and gnawed with great care, until she had separated five copies. After rewarding herself with a tasty lick of glue, she closed the pictures gently between her teeth, trotted to the edge of the desk, opened her mouth, and watched them flutter to the rug below.

For her own descent, Mary ran to the back of the black talking box, gripped its thick cord loosely in her paws, and slid—this part was fun!—back to the rug. There she collected the pictures, stacked them neatly for transport, and began her return journey to the colony, which she would enter via the room's south portal, a few mousetails east of the corridor doorway.

Up till this point, Mary's mission had played out according to plan.

But now it began to unravel.

Halfway across the room, she sensed a warning tingle in her whiskers, raised her snout, and caught the terrible scent of...the predator.

There followed simultaneously a rush of energy—*run!*—and a tide of tangled unhelpful thoughts: *What went wrong? How could the PWS have failed?*

With an effort, Mary steadied herself. To survive, she must act coolly and sensibly, first dropping the pictures so she could move fast, second identifying a new escape route.

It took Mary only a few seconds to evaluate her options, but in that time there arose a complication: A full-grown human resident of the shelter, the one called Matron Polly, was approaching along the corridor.

Apparently, the predator heard Matron, too, because he looked up, arched his back, mewed beseechingly, and voiced the rumble typical of his species—the one that silly humans found endearing.

"What are you doing down here, worthless? Did the boss lock you out again?" Matron Polly bent down to stroke him, and the rumbling grew louder.

Bleccch, thought Mary. *Sickening.* At the same time, she saw he was distracted, which created an opportunity for her. Over distance the predator—old as he was—had a speed advantage, making the portal from which she had come too far away. Her only chance was to race for the south portal, her original goal.

Mary ran as she had never run before, expecting when she reached the cracked molding at the base of the wall that she'd momentarily cross into the safety of mouse territory. Instead—*Oh, heartbreak*—her nose bumped a barrier blocking the opening from within.

Something had happened! She was closed out!

Mary suppressed her questions. She had one chance left, and it was a long shot. If she ran straight at the predator, his confusion might give her time to slip behind him and into the corridor. There was a backup portal there, only a few mouse-tails distant.

At first Mary's plan worked well. Apparently puzzled by the mouse's maneuver and encumbered by the human hand on his back, the predator tried to pounce and missed. Meanwhile, Matron Polly was too sleepy and slow either to see the soft gray interloper or to grasp the significance of the cat's behavior.

But then…disaster. This portal, too, was blocked, and now Mary was stranded with no escape from the malicious beast. Worst of all, she stood out in the open, in full view of the human.

Matron Polly shrieked. Down the hallway, a door opened. "What's the matter?"

Mary had just had time to recognize that this new voice belonged to a human pup when the predator pounced again. This time his weight knocked her forward at the same time that his claws ripped her shoulder. Barely a heartbeat later, she was upside down and staring into a merciless pink maw.

Mary had let down her dear, dear pups. Any second, sharp teeth would crunch her throat and they would be orphans... and she would be gone.

But then—just as the end seemed certain—Mary felt her stomach lurch and her body ascend. It was a moment before she realized what had happened, realized sharp teeth might have been preferable...for now her situation was truly terrifying. She was trapped in the dry, warm hand of a human pup.

Chapter Seven

"Scat now, Gallico, scat!" Caro McKay bumped the fat old thing with her foot. "The poor little mousie's terrified, and anyway he wouldn't be good for you, all raw the way he is. Now, mousie." The soft gray creature, which had been trembling, began to settle down in her hand. "What are we going to do about those scratches?"

"How can you touch that nasty thing, Caro?" Matron Polly made a face. "You're too kindhearted, you are. Wait till I tell Mrs. George, she'll have the exterminator in right quick. Don't be a fool, now, go on and flush him! Then wash your hands with lye soap."

Matron Polly was on the far side of middle age, doughy faced and pale except for spots of pink on her cheeks and the tip of her nose. She rarely smiled or frowned, but squinted constantly as if she were trying (and failing) to solve some conundrum.

Like all the intermediate girls, Caro knew better than to argue with Matron Polly. The more effective strategy was to agree, then do whatever you wanted. "Yes, ma'am. Good night, ma'am."

"And good night to you, too, then." Matron Polly took a

last look at the mouse, shivered, and turned to go back to her own room.

Caro cupped the mouse in her good hand, the left one, and followed Matron for a few steps before turning right into the girls' washroom. There she did not flush the mouse, but gripped it gently and cleaned its wounds with a damp paper towel.

"Mrs. George wouldn't like me nursing you, mousie. She can't abide mice, and if Matron remembers to tell her, she'll call the exterminator for sure. But I don't mind mice. You're just small creatures trying to get along, same as us kids."

As always, it was awkward trying to work with her scarred right hand, but it wasn't as painful as it used to be. Caro's handwriting was getting better, too. That was what Miss Ragone said.

Soon the mouse's wounds were clean, and Caro took a new paper towel to dry the fur. Then, securing the animal gently in her grip, she held it up and looked into its shiny black eyes. Maybe she was partial, having rescued it, but the mouse did seem to be unusually pretty—nose delicately pointed, whiskers pure white, ears like pink half-moons.

Caro thought of a book Miss Ragone had read to them. In it, a mouse named Stuart Little was born to a human family, fell in love with a bird, sailed in a mouse-sized boat, and drove an invisible car.

Stuart could talk and had an extensive wardrobe. He was smart and thoughtful. Of course it was a made-up story, but it stood to reason there was truth in it, too. Animals felt some things—hunger, for sure, and fear. Happiness? Maybe that, too.

"How is it being a mouse?" Caro asked.

The mouse tilted its head as if considering the question, then squeaked, making Caro laugh.

"Are you wondering what it's like to be a human? It's okay, I guess, for us kids that live here, at least. We've got enough to eat and clean clothes, but there was a war not very long ago, and people died, and over there in Europe and the Far East now there're those that don't have anything. Anyway, we don't have to worry about getting stomped or eaten the way you do—so that's something."

The mouse shifted in Caro's hand, then flicked its tail against her fingers. Caro understood at once, or thought she did. "You have to get home, don't you? Maybe you've got children waiting. Be good to them if you do. I'm an orphan, mousie. Do you know what that is? A kid who doesn't have a mother or a father. This place is a home for orphans."

Caro bumped the washroom door open with her hip and stood in the corridor. She had thought she would set the mouse free outdoors, but now she realized she'd wake someone if she tried that. So she knelt, opened her hand, and tipped the mouse out.

"All right, then," she said. "Get going back home now. I'll watch for that old cat and keep it away if I have to."

On the floor, the mouse looked around to orient itself,

then, to Caro's surprise, turned back to face her, lifted its snout, and squeaked.

"You're welcome," Caro said. "Nice to have met you, too." Then, because it seemed right, she raised her left pinkie finger and waved good-bye.

For its part, the mouse turned, flipped its tail, and scurried off.

With the cat nowhere to be seen, Caro went back to the washroom to wash her hands, glancing in the mirror as she did so.

Even apart from the scars, Caro knew she wasn't pretty. Her face was too square, nose too long, pale-brown hair too thick and wavy.

But, darn it, she was good. Too good, the other intermediates claimed—too studious, too obedient, too nice, even; entirely lacking in spunk.

Caro turned off the water, pulled down a paper towel, and dried her hands.

Well, wouldn't they all be surprised, she thought, *if they knew I got up in the middle of the night and talked to mice?*

Chapter Eight

Mary reentered mouse territory through the portal in the foyer, a chipped piece of marble behind a potted palm. She had no time to think about her "conversation" with the human pup or its odd behavior. She had more pressing concerns. By this time, she would have been reported overdue, and the colony scouts would be on alert. Sure enough, moments after her return, a squad intercepted her.

Their leader asked questions, which Mary did her best to answer before being overwhelmed by the pain in her shoulder. "Please, Nephew, may I have a chance to rest?" she asked.

The squad leader was firm. "You know the procedure. You have been seen. You must make your report straightaway."

"Are you detaining me?" Mary asked.

"Of course not, Auntie." The squad leader softened his tone. "What we're doing is escorting you to meet with Chief Director Randolph."

Mary's injuries were obvious and bloody. Even so, Randolph did not express concern. "What happened? Where are the pictures?" was his greeting.

As Mary began her report, Randolph's whiskers drooped. "Left on the rug in the boss's office?" he said. "And what happened next? You're back, so apparently the predator didn't eat you."

Mary ignored his callousness. "I followed protocol. I would have gotten away. But the south office portal was closed, and so was the one in the west corridor. Some mouse must have blocked them."

"Blocked them?" Randolph blinked. "That's preposterous."

Mary's mind was clear in spite of the pain. "No more preposterous than the failure of the PWS," she said. "How is it that the predator was on the loose when the monitors reported he was safely confined?"

"How should I know?" Randolph blustered. "It happens. Probably the boss was fed up and chased him out. What is it you're alleging, exactly?"

Mary was surprised. "I'm not alleging anything! But the PWS failed. And two portals were blocked. There should be an investigation. And I can't help thinking—" Her voice broke off.

"Thinking what?" Randolph said.

"Thinking something similar may explain what happened to Zelinsky."

Mary's tone had been mild. Randolph's response was explosive. "Nonsense! Wild-eyed speculation! Poppycock!"

The chief director's outburst provoked nervous glances among the scouts who had brought Mary to his nest. Seeing this, Randolph moderated his tone "What happened next?"

Now came the crux of Mary's report. She had been seen. More than that, she had been touched.

At this revelation, Randolph exploded anew. "A human pup held you in its paw?" His eyes flashed. "I should have known! I caught the stench of human but thought it was only because you'd been abroad in their territory."

"It was a female, and she saved my life," Mary said.

"Then released you?" Randolph was incredulous.

"There is something else," Mary said unhappily, "something more important. Both the pup—Caro—and Matron Polly mentioned the possibility of...an exterminator."

When Randolph heard this, the pink drained from his nose and ears. He did not speak for several seconds, and when he did, his voice was changed. "I see. It would seem, in that case, that the human pup's actions may have been a trick. She may have been using you to locate one of our portals. With this knowledge, she'll assist the exterminator in his work."

"No!" Mary defended Caro. "She didn't follow me—she didn't! I...I liked her."

Randolph ignored Mary's protest and turned to the squad leader. "Bring me the messenger on duty. The directors must meet at once. The talk of an exterminator, the human pup's strange behavior, the thief's fraternizing—all pose an imminent threat to the colony."

"Yes, Uncle," said the scout.

"As for you—Randolph looked at Mary—relieved of your duties. Confined to your nest. A guard will be placed there until you're called to testify."

Chapter Nine

Randolph's critics were right. The chief director was greedy, and he had long outstayed his usefulness. What they didn't realize was that Randolph knew all this himself. And he further knew that as a result, his hold on power was tenuous.

A better mouse would have given up his post and retired into respectable obscurity.

But Randolph liked being chief director.

He liked the way all the other mice had to be nice and pretend to like him. He liked ordering every mouse around. Most of all, he liked his pictures. Unlike pups or mates or subordinates, his pictures expected nothing and demanded nothing. They were faithful, constant, and beautiful. Other mice might make fun of him behind his back, but no mouse made fun of his pictures. Indeed, they wanted his pictures for their own.

No, Randolph wasn't ready to retire. And this was why, in recent months, he had resorted to extraordinary measures to protect his job. For example, when word had reached him that dissatisfied mice were organizing a Zelinsky takeover, he had spoken to some mice, who spoke to some mice, who put certain obstacles in the art thief's way the next time he embarked on a mission.

So much for Zelinsky.

Then, having seen that the art thief job might be a springboard to higher office—his own office—he had suggested the appointment of Mary Mouse. Old-fashioned himself, Randolph couldn't imagine any mouse taking seriously the idea of a female as chief director…until one day word reached him that times had changed, that he was wrong, that Mary Mouse might be a viable candidate in spite of her gender.

All right, then. No problem. Randolph's scheme to undermine Zelinsky had worked perfectly. There was every reason to think the same scheme would work again.

Only it hadn't. Instead, Mary Mouse had been seen by humans. The exterminator had been mentioned.

And now Randolph faced an awful prospect. The life he loved was over. Because of his own machinations, he, Randolph, would not only have to abandon his precious pictures, he would have to bring his mice through the colony's most severe crisis since its ancestors had migrated to Cherry Street from the Delaware River docks some fifty generations before.

Randolph had many qualities desirable in a leader. He was intelligent, resolute, well organized, and—born with an unusually resonant squeak—a persuasive speaker. Now, having gotten himself and every other mouse into this dire predicament, he determined he would get them out…or die trying.

And the first order of business was to drag his sorry bulk down from his divan, out of his nest, along the main pathway, and up the plumbing to the directors' chambers on the second floor.

Chapter Ten

The business of the emergency meeting of the Cherry Street directorate was soon accomplished. Once Mary had given her testimony, Randolph and his four colleagues agreed on the nature of the threat and the need for quick action. The challenges of moving more than a thousand mice were daunting, and thereafter most of the meeting was given over to logistical considerations.

As for Mary Mouse, Randolph committed one more act of perfidy when he convinced the other directors that her ineptitude and bad judgment had brought down calamity on them all. In Randolph's defense, he could hardly have told the truth. If he had, he would have been overthrown on the spot, leaving the colony leaderless in its darkest hour. Likewise, he could hardly have kept Mary around. Her insistence on an investigation into both her own thwarted mission and her mate's disappearance would pose an ongoing threat to his authority.

So it was that even though Mary was virtuous, smart, popular, and a mother—even though she had right on her side—she was sacrificed, her punishment the harshest possible in the world of mice: exile. Every other mouse in the colony would emigrate, including her own pups. She would be left behind. It was a sad fate made sadder still by the impending visit of the exterminator. Effectively, Mary had been sentenced to death.

Chapter Eleven

—◆—

Coming as a bolt from the blue to every mouse in the colony, the emigration order was met initially with confusion and pockets of defiance. These Randolph overcame by giving every mouse a job to do, thus uniting them to face the crisis.

With no time to waste, scouts departed and fanned out across the neighborhood, visiting alternative shelters one after another until at last they identified one that met the criteria for habitation: no existing rodent population, no residual extermination poisons, and minimal resident predators, all well fed.

It went without saying that the shelter must also be inhabited by humans because humans provide mice with all their essential comforts: comestibles, nesting materials, and winter warmth.

With the scouts' report complete, the directors approved preparations for settlement, and spies were dispatched to assess the human inhabitants' conversation, foragers to begin stocking the larders, builders to develop nests and pathways, garbage managers to identify sites for refuse, auditors to learn where stories were told, and, of course, an art thief to locate the source of pictures.

The thief, young and untried, had previously served as a scout. He had the agility required for the job, and no one doubted his intelligence, but his temperament was an open question. For his part, he would have liked to interview the colony's only living thief, Mary Mouse, to learn from her experience. But this Randolph forbade absolutely.

Chapter Twelve

On Sunday night another resident of the Cherry Street Children's Home—this one human—tossed and turned in her bed. This resident had lately learned there were mice sharing her roof, but that wasn't what disturbed her. Rather, Mrs. Helen George was apprehensive about the visitor expected in the morning.

It took a lot to impress Helen George. In her role as headmistress of an institution founded by prominent members of Philadelphia society, she was accustomed to meeting well-to-do people. But tomorrow's visitor was special, a bona fide movie star under contract to Paramount and featured only five months before on the cover of *Silver Screen* magazine.

Joanna Grahame was a hometown girl, born Gianna Garibaldi in South Philly, where she graduated from Catholic schools and then—to her parents' consternation—moved to New York City to become an actress. When a Hollywood director happened to see her in a bit part on Broadway, her career took off. That had been fifteen years before. Since then, she had starred in two dozen movies, had been linked romantically to multiple leading men, and had been married and divorced twice—once to a screenwriter (he drank) and once to a war hero (he drank, too).

Ordinarily, a celebrity's visit to the Cherry Street Home was exploited by both parties for its publicity value. After all, what Page 1 editor could resist the combination of cute orphans and glamor? But this visit was being kept quiet, at least for the time being. Both Miss Grahame and Mrs. George had their reasons. It might be that, if everything went well, there would be some future opportunity for mutually beneficial flashbulbs and mentions in the gossip column.

Helen George was beautiful but no longer young. At her dressing table early Monday morning, she concealed the effects of her insomnia with a deft application of face powder, fixed her silver hair into a French twist, aimed an aerosol can of hairspray, closed her eyes, and depressed the button.

Napping on the pink satin bedspread, her tabby cat heard the *sssss*, awoke, and swiped his paw across his nose, annoyed by the nasty smell.

Mrs. George caught sight of the cat's reflection, which reminded her of another responsibility. She needed to telephone the exterminator.

"What kind of cat doesn't kill mice?" she said to the tabby. "I brought you indoors because you're pretty, but that doesn't let you off the hook. You're lazy, is what you are."

The cat yawned, which seemed to confirm her assessment.

Mrs. George sighed. She didn't like calling the exterminator. When he came to do his dirty work, the staff and the children would have to leave the premises, and where were they to go? If mice had come to light the year before, the children could have gone to a municipal swimming pool, but not this summer, not when the rumor of polio was everywhere. Mrs. George couldn't afford to have a child get sick. That kind of publicity would be ruinous.

The headmistress's private apartment was on the third floor of the Cherry Street Home. Now, dressed in a pale-blue linen suit, Mrs. George locked her door, descended two flights of stairs, and turned left into the kitchen. There Mrs. Spinelli was preparing eggs, toast, and milk for the children.

Two of the intermediate girls, Barbara and Ginny, were helping and curtsied when they saw Mrs. George. "Morning, ma'am."

"Good morning, girls. Mrs. Spinelli?"

"Yes, ma'am." Unsmiling, Mrs. Spinelli presented Mrs. George with her coffee in a china cup on a saucer.

"Thank you," said Mrs. George.

"Mmph," said Mrs. Spinelli.

Mrs. George left the kitchen through the dining room, crossed the foyer, and entered her office, a large room on the same corridor as the girls' dormitories. On her desk, she found—as always—the *Philadelphia Inquirer*. Vaguely aware of the sounds coming from down the corridor, sounds made by girls arising, washing their faces, and dressing, Mrs. George sat down, arranged the newspaper in front of her, sipped her coffee, and read.

A worrisome front-page story about city politics caught her eye. A reformist candidate was trying to unseat the longtime Philadelphia sheriff, a powerful man who had done favors for

Mrs. George and her good friend Judge Jonathan Mewhinney. This push from the reformers might in turn cause her to hasten completion of her latest plan. If she expected to succeed, she would need perfect execution and a bit of luck.

Mrs. George drank the last of the now-tepid coffee, folded the newspaper…and then did something strange: looked around to be sure no one was watching. No one was. No one could have been, given the situation of her office in the west wing of the building. But what she was about to do required so much secrecy that she was superstitious in her caution.

Satisfied she was alone, Mrs. George removed two fifty-dollar bills from an inside pocket of her jacket and put each in a business envelope. Then she picked up the ivory-inlaid box on her desk, pulled open a hidden compartment, removed a tiny silver key, and used it to open a file drawer. From that drawer she took out an accounts ledger. It was not the one she shared with the Cherry Street Home's board of directors, but a second kept for her own use.

In the ledger, she noted the two fifty-dollar expenses but left blank the spaces for the dates they were incurred. Then she returned the book to the drawer, locked it, and put the key away. The envelopes she placed in her pocketbook in case she needed them on short notice.

It was eight-thirty, time to make her daily announcements at the children's breakfast table. The newspapers could be kept in the dark about the morning's visitor, but the children and the staff would have to be told.

Chapter Thirteen

All the children were delighted by Mrs. George's announcement, none more so than thirteen-year-old Melissa: "Joanna Grahame's coming here? *Good golly!*"

What would the movie star be wearing? Was she as beautiful in real life as she was on-screen? Would she bring along a handsome beau?

Melissa, who was tall, skinny, blond, and blue-eyed, rolled her eyes at that last question. "Don't be silly, Ginny. The whole world knows Joanna Grahame hasn't got a beau. She is done with romance. Her heart has been through the wringer once too often."

Betty, an intermediate like Ginny, tsked and shook her head. "You talk like one of those movie magazines."

"Of course she does, that's all she reads," said Ginny.

"That and comic books," said Bert.

"Don't make fun," said Caro.

"Yeah, Bert, 'cause you don't read at all," said Melissa.

Next to Caro at the table was four-year-old Annabelle. She had never seen a motion picture or till now heard the word *glamour*, but still she felt the excitement.

"Is Joanna Grahame a princess?" she whispered to Caro.

"Sort of," Caro said. "Only her mother isn't a queen."

"My mother isn't a queen," said Annabelle thoughtfully. "So can I be a princess?"

Across the table, Ricky heard her and snorted. "You haven't got a mother, or a father, either." At fifteen, Ricky had been at Cherry Street longer than any of the other children present. On his sixteenth birthday, he'd be released for good to make his way in the world.

"Have, too, got a mother," said Annabelle stoutly. "She's dead. But I've still got her. There's a picture in a frame."

This flummoxed Ricky, and Caro jumped in. "You can playact you're a princess," she told Annabelle. "That's what movie stars do. They pretend to be other people and get paid lots of money."

Jimmy Levine's seat was next to Ricky's. "It's a good racket, all right," he said. "Excuse me, ma'am. Mrs. George?"

"What is it, Jimmy?" Mrs. George had let the children chatter longer than usual.

"I presume our chores are canceled? Under the circumstances, I mean?"

"On the contrary," said Mrs. George. "Miss Grahame is arriving in her automobile at eleven. We'll want our home looking its best, and you have plenty of time to do chores. Annabelle—there's jam on your nose."

"Yes, ma'am." Annabelle touched her tongue to the spot without effect.

"Carolyn?" said Mrs. George.

"Yes, ma'am." Caro took the tip of her napkin and wiped Annabelle's nose.

"Can I ask a question, ma'am?" said Louisa, who was six. "Will the movie star make a movie about us?"

"She doesn't make the movies, she just acts in them," said Angela, another of the older girls.

"That's correct," said Mrs. George. "But you never know, Louisa. A movie about a nice home like ours, a home with happy children, would be refreshing."

Mrs. George never called the Cherry Street Home an orphanage. To her, the word denoted sickly children with hollow eyes who were beaten and fed gruel. Cherry Street was nothing like that. Rather, it had been established by Mr. and Mrs. C. Philips-Bodbetter in 1936 to model the most progressive methods for rearing abandoned children of all races, creeds, and backgrounds.

A kind couple who had made their fortune manufacturing baby powder, the Philips-Bodbetters were much too busy to run the home themselves. For advice on management, they turned to a lawyer friend, who suggested an attractive widow to serve as headmistress. At the interview, the widow showed herself to be so self-possessed, so well-spoken, and so obviously capable that they hired her after only the most cursory check into her background.

Similarly impressed, the newly constituted board of directors left it to Mrs. George—for she was the widow—to hire the staff.

The girls' matron, Polly Merkel, was an old acquaintance of Mrs. George's who had been on the job from the beginning. Over the years, half a dozen boys' supervisors had come and gone. The current one, Donald Cleary, had been employed since shortly after his army discharge.

Pleasant though it was, the Cherry Street Home was still an orphanage. The food was sufficient and nourishing but not delicious—canned vegetables; canned fruit; meat on Sundays, Tuesdays, and Thursdays; margarine in place of butter; and lots of potatoes, bread, noodles, and rice.

The children wore donated shoes and clothes, mostly secondhand, and slept four or six to a room. Each child had a single cupboard in which to store possessions, the most prized of which—for those lucky enough to have them—were photographs, tangible signs that once they had been like other children, once they had had a family.

In the summer of 1949, there were twenty boys and eighteen girls in residence, with Ricky the oldest and Annabelle the youngest. Besides the dormitories, there was a baby nursery at the west end of the second-floor corridor, but it was rarely occupied. The Cherry Street Home was not staffed for full-time care of children under age three, and babies stayed only briefly en route to more permanent situations.

Now, morning announcements over, the younger boys got up to clear the dishes. After that, the children dispersed—first to visit the washrooms, then to begin their chores.

By this time both the excitement and the noise level

had subsided. If anything, the children were more thought-ful than usual, all wondering the same thing: What if Joanna Grahame was visiting for a particular reason that Mrs. George didn't mention? What if she wanted to adopt one of them for her own?

Chapter Fourteen

———◆———

Each week the chore chart rotated, and each Sunday evening Caro checked to learn the next day's assignment. Monday morning's was easy: clean the main parlor. Her partner was the star-struck Melissa, and the two dusted and mopped side by side.

"Will Miss Grahame bring us presents, do you think?" Melissa asked after they'd been working for a while. "Maybe perfume or chocolates or a mink coat…" Her voice trailed off dreamily.

Caro laughed. "A mink coat? What would you even do with one?"

"Wear it, of course!" said Melissa. "I'd put it on right now."

"To clean the parlor in August?" Caro said.

Melissa amended her request. "A silk gown, and high-heeled shoes like Betty Grable's. Do you think Miss Grahame knows Betty Grable?"

Caro shrugged. "She's bound to, I guess. All those famous stars in Hollywood probably pal around."

Melissa nodded. "And do nothing all day but get dressed in their silk clothes and style their hair and eat caviar and go to parties."

"Caviar's just fish eggs," said Caro.

Melissa made a face. "That's not true."

"It is," said Caro. "I read it someplace. And besides, those Hollywood stars have to work, too, so they can afford fish eggs and nice clothes."

"Work? Ha!" said Melissa. "I could be a movie star, easy. You just stand in front of a big camera and say the words they tell you." She struck a pose. "Oh! My darling, my darling! How I do love you so!" Melissa wrapped herself in her own embrace, closed her eyes, and puckered her lips—*kiss, kiss, kiss.*

Caro laughed. She liked Melissa. She was lazy but also funny, and she could imitate people's voices, too. Sometimes in the washroom she playacted Mrs. George, and all the girls howled with laughter.

Like a lot of the children at Cherry Street, Melissa was not a true orphan. Rather, she had been an extra mouth to feed in a big family without means. One day, overwhelmed by responsibilities he couldn't meet, her father had gone out for cigarettes and never returned. When Melissa first arrived, she wouldn't talk about herself. Whether it was because their families didn't want them, were poor, or didn't exist, new arrivals were often ashamed.

Eventually, though, they woke up to realize that everyone else was in the same predicament. They were "a bunch of poor unloved rejects," according to Ricky. And so, over time, Melissa, like the others, had found her place.

"Maybe you should audition for Miss Joanna Grahame," Caro told Melissa.

"Maybe I should." Melissa reached for the polishing rag, only to see that Caro had already finished with it. "There, you've gone and done my work for me again."

"Fancy that," said Caro. "Come on. It's ten to eleven."

Caro and Melissa untied their aprons, returned the cleaning supplies, and hurried to the washroom, where the other intermediate girls—Barbara, Betty, and Ginny—stood at the sinks, toweling off their scrubbed faces.

There was a good deal of noise in the washroom, a little pushing, moderate amounts of splashing, and some scrutinizing of blemishes in the mirror before—with one minute to spare—the girls raced down the corridor to the foyer, a grand room with a marble floor, a domed ceiling, and a far-off chandelier, to await the arrival of Joanna Grahame.

Chapter Fifteen

Mr. Donald and Matron Polly did their best to keep the children quiet and in order, but it was a losing battle. First Billy and Louisa made faces at each other and giggled, then one of the boys, probably fourteen-year-old Ned, made a rude noise, causing all the boys to laugh and all the girls to roll their eyes, sigh, and shake their heads.

Just as things threatened to get altogether out of control, the double doors opened wide to reveal—backlit by sunshine—the movie star herself.

"Children?" Mrs. George said. "May I introduce a new friend of Cherry Street? This is Miss Joanna Grahame."

"Good morning, children!" Miss Grahame greeted them.

"Good morning, miss," the children replied.

She was beautiful in the thin-lipped, strong-jawed way that had become popular during the war. Her dark-gold hair was straight and shoulder-length. She wore a snug pale-pink suit, matching gloves, and a hat crowned by a single black feather. She carried a pink patent leather pocketbook.

The children watched in awe as Joanna Grahame tugged her gloves from her hands and made her way into the room, smiling her marquee-strength smile. Her movements were so straight-backed, elegant, and purposeful that Mrs. George, trailing in her wake, seemed diminished.

Caro had always thought of herself as supremely sensible; certainly not star-struck like Melissa. Now, regarding a movie star for the first time, she felt her knees weaken. She had never seen anyone so beautiful. If only she could be like her. If only there were a magic wand powerful enough to make that transformation.

The actress did not greet every child but only the ones who struck her fancy. She would have passed Caro right by,

but Mrs. George directed her attention. "I'd like you to meet one of our finest young ladies, Miss Grahame," she said. "This is Carolyn McKay."

Miss Grahame turned, met Caro's eye, and held out her hand.

Caro blanched.

How could she have failed to anticipate this?

There was nothing to be done, though. She held her hand out in return; the star grasped it automatically…and her smile turned to an expression of disgust. "Oh!" She looked at Caro's misshapen fingers, the angry pink-and-white scars that reached almost to her elbow. Then she pulled away and snapped at Mrs. George, "Well, you might've warned me!"

For one, two, three heartbeats, the room was silent but for the ugly comment's reverberations. Then Mrs. George cooed something apologetic, and Miss Grahame—after wiping her offended hand on her skirt—moved on to greet Annabelle, who was so flustered that she burst out crying.

This brought Miss Grahame up short. "Gee whiz!"

Mrs. George recovered her poise. "Perhaps we'd better go upstairs to see the classrooms."

"Yeah, let's," said Miss Grahame.

A moment later, when the two grand ladies were gone, Caro willed herself to breathe…and breathed. Her tears were not so obedient. Even though she closed her eyes, she could not stop them.

Matron Polly tried to soothe her crying. And Mr. Donald.

51

And Jimmy, her best friend, who called Miss Grahame an "old cow," and Melissa, who said she'd never go to see another of her pictures, not if she lived to be a hundred.

It was Annabelle who snapped her out of it. Annabelle needed her. Blubbering inconsolably, she tugged on Caro's blouse till Caro picked her up and—ignoring the damp combination of baby tears and snot—squeezed her to her shoulder.

"If that mean lady's a princess," Annabelle whispered in Caro's ear, "then I don't wanna be one."

Chapter Sixteen

———⟫◆⟪———

Mrs. George was disgusted with Miss Grahame for hurting Carolyn's feelings. She would have to fix things, but right off the bat did not know how. The next two days were full of appointments, including one with her helpful friend, the sheriff. In the evenings, Judge Mewhinney would visit as usual. But—as soon as she could find a moment—she would have a word with Carolyn.

For now, though, her principal concern was to keep this foolish woman happy.

"Upstairs I'll show you the classrooms, and then we'll come back to the children's dormitories. Does that suit you?" Mrs. George asked Miss Grahame as the two ascended the main staircase.

Miss Grahame nodded absently. "Okay, sure. Say, what happened to that little girl, anyway?"

"House fire," Mrs. George replied. "Her mother died, and Carolyn . . . well, as you see."

"And she doesn't have a daddy?" Miss Grahame asked.

"The war," said Mrs. George simply.

Miss Grahame nodded. "I see. Some kids don't have much

luck, do they? Still, I suppose she can get some kind of factory work, some line where her looks don't matter."

"She's very bright." Mrs. George suddenly felt protective. "Bright enough for higher education, I think. She would make a fine teacher."

Miss Grahame thought a moment, then shook her head. "Nah. She'd scare kids away with that red claw of hers. Better if she has a job that's more out-of-the-way-like. One thing's sure. She'll never find a husband."

Mrs. George did not reply. You couldn't call Carolyn attractive, but Mrs. George had realized she was special from the day they met. Frank Kittaning, the child welfare inspector, had brought her in for an interview, and six-year-old Carolyn had sat without once fidgeting, even though she must have been in great pain, her arm still swathed in bandages after the fire.

Carolyn had answered Mrs. George's questions in complete sentences. She hadn't smiled, but neither had she seemed sullen.

By that time, Mrs. George had been headmistress for eight years and knew a thing or two about how children get along. One thing she'd learned was that a certain type of responsible, sweet-tempered child could have a calming effect on the others. Carolyn would be just such a child, she was sure of it. And so—over time and out of Frank Kittaning's hearing—she had reframed the little girl's history in a way that ensured absolute loyalty to Mrs. George.

"If I hadn't spoken up, you might be living in some dirty orphanage without enough food to eat, someplace cold in winter and hot in summer, someplace where you didn't even get to go to school. You understand that, don't you?" Mrs. George had said.

"Yes, ma'am. I do. Thank you, ma'am."

"But I spoke to Mr. Kittaning. I told him I wanted you especially."

"Thank you, ma'am." Carolyn had said this gravely.

Mrs. George had told Caro much more than that—about the circumstances of the fire, how her mother had died, Caro's childish actions at that time—all stories spun deliberately, all stories Caro took to heart.

Five years later, she was indeed loyal to her benefactress, besides being popular with the other children, a combination that yielded precisely the pacific results Mrs. George had hoped for. As for Carolyn's scars, sometimes—like today, when she had thoughtlessly introduced Carolyn to Miss Grahame— Mrs. George forgot all about them.

It was a few minutes later in the older girls' dormitory when Miss Grahame turned to Mrs. George and said: "You know, I have so longed for a child of my own, a son. But fate has not seen fit to favor me." Then (the cue seemed to have been written into a script somewhere), she sighed.

The two women had been surveying beds and shoes—

lined up, well ordered, and pleasing to the eye. Mrs. George nodded sympathetically. "What a shame," she said with feeling, even though the fact was already known to her, indeed the reason for Miss Grahame's visit.

"And I, uh...understand," Miss Grahame went on, "that you're often the first to hear of babies, healthy babies, who are available for adoption?"

Mrs. George nodded. "Yes. It happens that unfortunate young women get themselves into trouble, or, in some cases, that families can't afford another mouth to feed."

"Where I live in California, the agencies will only give babies to married couples," Miss Grahame said. "An older kid I might be able to get, some kind of a desperate situation. But I say an older kid's already damaged goods, am I right? I want a new baby so I can start fresh, make it my own."

Mrs. George knew most people felt the same way; they just didn't express themselves so bluntly. Diplomatically, she replied, "I'm aware of the legal limitations, and of course, many children's societies have their own restrictions as well."

"But your place, Cherry Street. It's more lenient? At least, that's what I hear."

"I'm a widow myself," Mrs. George said, "and I believe a woman on her own is fully capable of raising a child. Furthermore, even though I've only known you this short while, I'm confident you'd make a wonderful mother."

Miss Grahame smiled, apparently confident as well. "So you can help me?"

"We have helped other women in your circumstances."

By now the two women had made their way to the headmistress's office. On entering, Mrs. George closed the door and invited her guest to sit down.

"And you'll help me," Miss Grahame insisted. It had been years since a wish of hers had been frustrated.

"There's the matter of the woman signing over parental rights, and a judge's approval. There will be expenses, and possibly certain additional fees, since yours is a special case." Mrs. George sat down behind her desk. "Now, from what you say, you're interested in a newborn boy? A newborn Caucasian boy?"

"Blond," said Miss Grahame, "so he looks like me."

Chapter Seventeen

In the summer, the children at the Cherry Street Home had their afternoons free for games, or reading, or playing outside. With so many playmates, there was always something to do.

On this evening, most of the children had listened to the RCA radio, newly purchased by Mr. and Mrs. Philips-Bodbetter. There were songs by Frankie Laine and the Andrews Sisters, and the new favorite serial drama, *Dragnet*. The combination of an exotic setting (Los Angeles!) with realistic police stories had proved irresistible.

Mr. Donald never missed an episode.

During the remainder of that bright, slow summer day, Caro had done her best to act normal...and had mostly succeeded, though Matron Polly noted her lack of appetite. The fact was, however, that Miss Grahame's remark had been devastating.

Caro was cheerful, reliable, and dutiful, but she was also a child like other children. She wanted to be pretty, and she never would be. She wished she had party clothes, and a dog of her very own, and books and toys and a canopy bed and a room she didn't have to share.

Most of all, she wished she had parents who loved her the

way only parents could, a mother and a father who thought she was special for one single solitary reason, because she was Caro.

She would never have any of those things, and most days she willed herself to believe that that was fine. But now that awful woman, that awful yet beautiful woman, had made a face and yanked her hand away—and just like that, a torrent of pent-up sadness had been let loose.

In the washroom before bed, the girls in the intermediate dormitory completed their dissection of the visit of Miss Joanna Grahame, which, they all agreed, had been a bust—even leaving aside her rudeness to Caro. She hadn't brought presents or shown the least interest in adopting one of them. And when you saw her close up—did you notice?—that hair of hers wasn't so blond at the roots, and she had crow's-feet.

Listening to the other girls' chatter, Caro had agreed when called upon to do so. Her own raw feelings she set aside.

Now, minutes before lights-out, Betty, Ginny, and Barbara were reading comic books in bed. Lying down, Caro decided she couldn't interest herself in either Archie or Superman, so she turned off her reading lamp and closed her eyes. The air in the room was sticky. Like the other girls, she lay on top of her sheets.

"You okay, Caro?" asked Betty, whose bed was closest.

"I'm okay," Caro answered, eyes still shut. "Thanks."

When at last Matron Polly opened the dormitory door and said, "Lights out, girls," Caro was alone in the dark. She was so exhausted, had so looked forward to this moment, that she drifted off immediately, only to suffer a long-forgotten dream: She was six years old and in her own house with her mother. It was a few days after the men wearing uniforms came to the door to tell them her soldier father—a hero, her mother said—was dead, killed in the desert at Kasserine Pass.

Ever since that day, her mother had been distracted, forgetful. That evening she had left a kettle on the stove till the water burned away and the red-hot metal ignited the wooden handle, setting the kitchen curtains ablaze.

In her dream, Caro saw it all, though she hadn't known the story at the time. It was Mrs. George who told her later. That day in the flames, all she knew was choking smoke and awful heat and then the blessed relief of breathing cool night air as she ran away, away, away—thinking only of herself, leaving her mother alone in the house to die.

Chapter Eighteen

While Caro slept, the mice made final preparations. It was after eleven when Randolph gave the order: *"First wave—depart!"* And with that, ten divisions of mice, each numbering between twenty and twenty-five, flowed from the shelter's cracks, gaps, and crannies into the deserted alley beyond.

Lit only by the moon and streetlamps, the spectacle was rousing—an infinity of ears, furry backsides, and tails in skittering, purposeful motion. Watching from his vantage at the base of a broken drain spout, Randolph felt both pride and terror. Some of these mice would lose their lives...to stray cats, dogs, and rats, unexpected owls, uncharted holes in the ground, automobiles, stomping human boots, and every other thing that imperils the smallest creatures.

The night progressed, and Randolph released the second, third, and fourth waves at intervals, measured by the angle of the shadows on the shelter's back wall. In all, more than one thousand mice would depart their nests—nests some families had occupied for a score of generations.

If resettlement proved a success—and there was every reason to think it would—the chief director who had greedily and unscrupulously clung to power (and pictures) would go down in history as the heroic leader who had saved the colony. The irony was not lost on the chief director himself.

While every other mouse rushed to complete preparations, Mary had been confined to her nest with plenty of time to think. What had gone wrong? Had someone deliberately sabotaged her mission? Had someone sabotaged Zelinsky's?

But as the hours passed, the futility of that line of inquiry became apparent and her thoughts shifted. She questioned her ambitions for Zelinsky and her decision to accept her own appointment as thief. She wished she had not secretly enjoyed the deference other mice showed her. She wondered if she had become arrogant.

Finally, her thoughts settled on the most important thing: her pups. She had let them down…and how would they get along? The directorate had assigned their care to an old auntie, but it would not be the same as having a mother.

With a start, Mary realized her own girls would now be in the same position as the human pups who lived at Cherry Street. The one who had rescued her from the predator, Caro her name was, she had called them orphans.

What a strange encounter that had been!

The human pup had asked how it was to be a mouse with such polite eagerness that Mary had felt obliged to answer: "Very pleasant most of the time."

She hadn't expected the human to understand. After eons of highly motivated practice, mice had learned human language, but humans had never got the knack of Mouse. Still,

Caro had shown unexpected aptitude, even replying appropriately when Mary had squeaked, "Thank you and good-bye!"

Mary wondered what had happened to Caro's mama and papa. Was she sad that they were gone? Did she miss them? Or maybe—and this would be worse yet—she didn't care anymore.

Randolph had many faults, but gratuitous cruelty was not one. Assigned to the final wave of migrants, Mary's three pups were given permission to visit their mother and say good-bye.

"What did you do wrong, Mama?" asked Millie.

"Why can't you come with us?" asked Matilda.

The questions stabbed Mary's heart.

"I don't know if I did anything wrong," she told her daughters honestly. "But bad things happen, and sometimes it's for no reason. When they do, I suppose, goodness must be its own consolation."

Millie and Matilda looked at each other and blinked. What was Mama talking about?

But Margaret—her anxious pup—understood a little.

"Tell us a story, Mama," Margaret said. "Tell us a story to make us feel better."

Mary did not believe there was such a story. But she began anyway: "Once upon a time," and the gift of a story was given. It was the last episode in the tale of Stuart Little, when the dapper young hero leaves behind a star-crossed romance, the town of Ames' Crossing, and a telephone company repairman to drive north into the great land that stretches before him, adventuring in search of his lost love, Margalo.

"Did he find her, Mama?" asked Millie.

"*Shhh*, silly, that's not the point," said Margaret.

"Seems like it ought to be the point," said Matilda.

"I don't know if Stuart found her," said Mary. "But he never stopped believing he would, and he never stopped trying."

Mary was going to say something wise about Stuart's quest, her own inadequate attempts at goodness, and the bravery all of them would need to face the future, but she heard a noise outside her nest; the guard was coming.

It would never do for her pups to worry about her. If they were to carry on with strength and confidence, they must think she was doing the same. So she arranged her ears, sat up straight on her haunches, and curled her tail neatly into a coil.

"Let us touch noses, each of us, one last time," she said. "Auntie Edna will take good care till you're out on your own. And think of me sometimes, please"—her voice caught—"just as you think of your papa."

Chapter Nineteen

———◆———

Emotionally exhausted, still suffering the consequences of the predator's attack, Mary Mouse slept hard that day and awoke with a start.

What time was it? Why had no one waked her? She was in her own familiar nest, but it was so quiet, and the comforting mousy aroma seemed thin.

Then she remembered. It was dusk, judging from the quality of light in the pathway outside, and she was alone. Every mouse she'd ever known was gone.

Mary indulged herself with a sigh, thinking of all she had lost and how unfair it was.

Then she got up, groomed her ears and paws, and trotted for breakfast to the nearest larder, where she beheld an awesome sight: morsels of every taste, color, and texture—salty, sweet and sour, crunchy, tender and chewy—all arranged in neat piles, and all for Mary.

"Why, of course," she said aloud. "They didn't have a way to carry the comestibles."

Gratefully, Mary inhaled the stale scent. It wasn't the same as companionship, but it was something.

Then she set about choosing her meal—a bit of salmon loaf,

half a lima bean, and a crumb each from a graham cracker and a gingersnap. When she wiped her whiskers, she was stuffed.

"But I mustn't always have two desserts," she told herself. "If there's any hope of my avoiding the exterminator, I have spying to do. And spying means climbing."

Every Cherry Street mouse knew that the best time for spying was in the evening around eight o'clock. That was when the boss's mate drove his automobile to the shelter, parked on the street, let himself in through the front door, climbed the stairs, and paid a visit during which he and the boss conversed while sipping amber-colored liquid.

The boss was not typically talkative, but during these conversations she had revealed many secrets useful to mice. A single mouse could not monitor the humans as thoroughly as a whole network of spies, so Mary was determined to take advantage of these nightly opportunities.

As far as mice are concerned, plumbing exists for the convenience of mice. Now Mary set out to climb the cold-water pipe to the boss's apartment, a full 180 mousetails distant. Climbing at her usual rate of twenty mousetails per minute (mpm), she ought to be there before the judge arrived.

But she hadn't considered her injured shoulder. It was still painful, and by the time she reached the second floor, she was breathless. She paused to recover herself and stretch, then commenced to climb again—never looking down.

Not for nothing do mice have big ears. It was the echo of

the scratch of paws on pipes that told Mary she'd achieved her goal. A moment later, she heard two distinct human voices. Judge Mewhinney—the boss's mate—had already arrived.

Mary dropped off the pipe, assessed her options and decided to squeezed through a hole that led to a cupboard. There she was in luck. The cupboard doors did not close tightly, and through the gap, she peered across the smooth floor of what appeared to be a kitchen and into the lighted parlor.

Mary sniffed, inhaling the scents of soap, floor wax, dust…and smoke from the judge's cigar. Like all mice, Mary hated and feared smoke. It was all she could do not to cough and attract the attention of the predator. She could smell him as well, and a fit of trembling assailed her. With a great effort of will, she mastered it. She had to spy if she was going to avoid the exterminator. She would be careful. She would stay out of sight. The predator would never know she was there.

The boss was speaking.

"…Polly's associate at the lying-in hospital…a blond male born today."

"And the mother?" Judge Mewhinney asked.

"Unwed," said the boss.

Judge Mewhinney's voice conveyed his smile. "A bit of luck, then. But are you prepared to act so quickly?"

"If the girl doesn't cooperate, I'll have to have a talk with our friend the sheriff," said Mrs. George. "And Polly may have to manage without a nurse. But on the whole, yes. I am prepared."

"What about Miss Grahame?" asked the judge.

"I've spoken to her private secretary. She seems to think a larger hotel suite and some baby formula are all that's required."

"So, smooth sailing, then." The judge puffed on his cigar, filling the small space with the acrid smell of smoke.

"I hope so," said Mrs. George, "but I don't want to keep the child a moment longer than we have to. It's not only Polly. I

68

don't like what I'm reading about the sheriff being challenged. Someone new might take a hard look at our operation."

"And put us out of business?" said the judge.

After that, the boss must have turned her head, because her words were muffled. Mary became fretful. For all she knew, the boss was naming the date for the exterminator! She had to be close enough to hear.

Silently, Mary squeezed through the gap between the doors, scurried across the linoleum, and hid beneath the cupboards' overhang. From there, she could see the boss's stockings and high heels, one of the judge's shiny brown shoes, and the back of his armchair.

Mary tried to concentrate on the conversation, but the word *exterminator* did not come up, and she was distracted by the stuffing in the armchair. It looked to be of excellent quality. Perhaps she should establish a winter home for herself here? It was warmer at high elevations.

The judge's feet shifted, recapturing Mary's attention. "Miss Grahame by all accounts is wealthy. How much this time?" he asked.

"Leave that to me," said Mrs. George.

"Helen, may I remind you I run a considerable risk?"

The boss's voice softened. "We both run a risk, my dear. And your contribution is invaluable. Still, it's better if you don't know every detail. What if you were questioned? With that new bunch trying to take over City Hall—"

"They wouldn't question *me*. Would they?" When his voice squeaked, the judge sounded almost like a mouse.

"Surely not. But it's better to be safe than sorry."

Still nothing about an exterminator, and Mary's mind had drifted back to the armchair stuffing and her winter home when all at once she realized that the judge had taken another puff on his cigar, and the smoke was tickling her throat, and she must retreat lest she make a noise to attract attention....

She started to turn but was too late. A single step, and the worst happened: Mary coughed.

Chapter Twenty

In Gallico's dream, he was tormenting the twitching tail of a vanquished lizard. It was lovely, which was why he felt more than the usual resentment when the rodent's sneeze awakened him.

The humans, oblivious to the impending drama continued their chatter. Really, it was amazing that humans ever accomplished anything, given their minimal sensory abilities. By rights, felines should run the world, with canine slaves providing muscle.

True to his species, Gallico was slow to rouse, but once on his feet moved quickly. In an instant, he was crouched and taking aim. *Stupid rodent*, he thought. *Does she think I can't see her there?*

Behind him, the boss said, "What is that cat up to, do you think?"

And the judge answered, "He's got his eye on something."

Gallico set his body and sprang, but the rodent made a last-second course adjustment and the cat came up a half claw short.

Now Gallico was mad. The boss had scolded him for failing to kill that female the other night—as if interference by a human kitten had somehow been his fault. The boss had also accused him of being lazy, which was ludicrous. How could she expect him to maintain his good looks without the requisite beauty sleep?

This time, Gallico would not fail. This time, no human kitten would come to the rescue. This time the rodent was on her own.

Chapter Twenty-One

Disoriented by fear and surprise, Mary sped across the floor and arrived at the wrong cupboard, one whose doors closed tightly enough that she could not slip between them. The predator was close now, so close she could smell its bloodthirsty breath even over the cigar smoke.

I'm done for, she thought. *No one cares about an exile. No one will even know I'm gone.*

But then...an image flashed in her mind, the hero Stuart Little facing down the wicked white feline, Snowbell. Miss Ragone had shown the picture to the children when she read the book aloud, and the mice auditors had seen it, too, and been impressed.

Stuart Little had overcome his fear. Stuart Little had not given up.

I won't, either, Mary thought. *The stupid beast's sheer size might prove decisive, but I will go down fighting.*

Emboldened, Mary wheeled to confront the predator head-on. She did not cower but placed her paws solidly, bared her not-inconsequential teeth, and flexed her muscles. Prepared to jump at the big brute's throat, she let out a ferocious squeak and—what do you know?—the furry coward flinched.

In the parlor, shoes shifted. "What was that noise? What's that cat up to?"

The human speech diverted the predator's attention, and Mary ran for it. This time she located the cupboard she wanted, squeezed between the doors, and arrived safe, enclosed, and in the dark—her heart pounding.

"Blast!" the boss said.

"More mice?" the judge asked.

And that was the last Mary heard before she grasped the cold-water pipe and, aided by gravity, sped down, down, down to mouse territory on the ground floor.

Chapter Twenty-Two

Mary couldn't exactly call her first spy mission successful.

She had learned nothing important.

She had nearly been eaten.

And while she wasn't sure the boss had seen her, the boss had certainly suspected her presence. If anything, extermination was more likely than ever now.

Mary Mouse was discouraged and exhausted. And the worst part was, she had to spy again the following day—every day—if she was to protect herself. Somehow she would have to find a way to hear what was said while steering clear of the predator.

For now, she deserved a snack.

She was rounding a corner on the pathway to the larder when she smelled something unexpected: fresh droppings that were not her own.

She stopped. She looked around. She spotted the source . . . and tried to explain it away. Maybe the droppings were older than they smelled? Maybe she just hadn't noticed them before?

But all the time, she knew the truth. An intruder had entered her territory. A male.

Historically, the Cherry Street colony had been forced to defend its shelter repeatedly against raids and even outright invasion. Under Randolph's predecessor, defensive capabilities had been improved such that the colony gained a reputation for impregnability, deterring any potential attack. While Mary herself had been born in an era of unprecedented peace, she knew that Randolph had allowed colony defenses to deteriorate.

Did the intruder represent a force hoping to conquer a poorly defended colony? Or did he know that Mary was in fact all alone?

Her mind in turmoil, Mary heard scuttling nearby, turned her head, and beheld an unfamiliar male with the wild look of the outdoors about him, rangy, muscular, and untidy compared to the males of the territory, who were well fed and committed to good grooming.

This was a marauder mouse for sure—a pirate, a raider, a dangerous outlaw. Squealing would be to no avail. Mary looked around for a weapon but found nothing useful.

Meanwhile, the male skipped the formalities. "As I live and breathe! You scared me half to death! But tell me, where has everyone got to?"

Mary hardly knew how to reply.

"Predator got your tongue? *Ha ha ha ha ha!*" said the male.

So okay, maybe this fellow wasn't the advance guard of an enemy force. In fact, he seemed more ridiculous than threatening. But he wasn't making a good impression, either. Mary looked him up and down, then raised her pure-white whiskers and gave the traditional greeting for a stranger: "Did you travel far?"

"*Ha ha ha ha ha!*" said the male. "How courteous you are. Yes, rather far. And there's no need to worry, my dear. I am not scouting an invasion. In fact, I am a member of the Cherry Street colony, same as—I infer—you are. So where'd everybody go, anyhow?"

Not wanting to reveal she was an exile, Mary answered with a question: "If you're a member of the colony, then why are you traveling alone?"

"I might ask why you're alone as well," said the male. "An outcast, are you? Not dangerous, I trust? You're right to be prudent, you know, a defenseless damsel in your position."

Mary arched her back, raised her hackles, and glared. Who was he to call her a defenseless damsel? Hadn't she just faced down a predator?

Her assertive posture did not have the desired effect. In fact, it was met with another blaring "*Ha ha ha ha ha!*" followed by "Look, can we go somewhere to chat? There's hours yet till daylight, and I'd love to get off my paws. I'll be glad to tell you where I came from, my whole life story. But just now I'm peckish, and from the looks of the larder—I hope you don't mind that I peeked—you're admirably stocked with comestibles."

Hmph, Mary thought. *And yet—maybe I've misjudged him? An uncivilized rodent would have eaten first and asked questions later.* "Yes, of course. You must forgive my manners. My name is Mary Mouse."

The male raised his whiskers and dipped his snout. "My name," he said, "is Andrew."

Chapter Twenty-Three

While Mary and the intruder chatted, Mrs. George slept. In the morning, she came downstairs as usual, sat at her desk with her coffee and newspaper, and prepared to face the challenges of the coming day. Among her talents was lying, and this morning she would put that talent to use. Later, she would make time at last to meet privately with Carolyn.

From Matron, Mrs. George knew that Carolyn had not been her usual cheerful self since the insult—and this would not do. The children relied on Carolyn's good humor. And so did Mrs. George.

How to make the child feel better? How to restore her confidence?

Mulling over these questions, Mrs. George had an idea that made her smile. Maybe the lack of a baby nurse would not be so hard on Polly after all. Carolyn had a maternal streak. It was one of the qualities that drew the other children to her. The coincidence, she thought, just might work out very neatly.

As usual after breakfast, Mrs. George made her announcements to the staff and the children. Then she set the time to meet with Carolyn and returned to her office with Matron Polly. There the two reviewed the schedule at the lying-in hospital. It was eight-fifteen now; healthy babies were brought to their mothers for nursing between nine and ten. It would take Mrs. George fifteen minutes by car to get to the hospital. Polly's associate would meet her outside.

From her wallet, Mrs. George withdrew the envelopes she had prepared Monday morning and gave them to the matron, who put them in the pocket of her apron. "Thank you, ma'am," she said, but there was a frown on her face.

Mrs. George raised her eyebrows. "I've given you what we agreed on."

"Yes, ma'am. Only... well, it's a nasty business, and—"

Mrs. George cut her off. "This is an inopportune time to lose heart, Polly. We have done this before."

"Yes, ma'am."

"We are giving the child an opportunity."

Polly did not look certain but repeated, "Yes, ma'am."

Polly and Mrs. George had first become acquainted two decades before, shortly after Mrs. George moved to Philadelphia. At the time, Polly was the young and foolish girlfriend of a speakeasy's proprietor. When she became pregnant, he departed for parts unknown, never knowing his baby had been miscarried.

Polly was heartbroken at the loss of her beau and the loss of her child. Her life improved when Mrs. George became headmistress at Cherry Street and invited her to live in and oversee the girls. Mrs. George rightly anticipated that Polly's placid disposition was well suited to working with children... and to working for Mrs. George.

Mrs. George had endured Polly's second thoughts before. Now she spoke firmly. "You and the nurse have earned your money. At the same time, should you ever be tempted to tell what you know, you can expect the authorities to deal with you harshly. Not everyone sees our enterprise in its proper light."

Matron Polly swallowed. "No, ma'am."

"Is the nursery ready?" asked Mrs. George.

"Nearly."

"Go and finish up with it, then. I'll be back before lunchtime."

Chapter Twenty-Four

Shortly after nine o'clock, Mrs. George drove her Nash sedan across the Schuylkill River to the lying-in hospital in West Philadelphia. The sky was blue and the air not so humid as usual. Mrs. George's white dress and jacket, which resembled a nurse's uniform, remained crisp and professional.

In 1949 most women delivered their babies in hospitals, just as they do today. Other details, however, were quite different. In the special hospitals for mothers and babies, which were called maternity or lying-in hospitals, the doctors were all men and the nurses all women. After delivery, mother and baby typically remained hospitalized for an entire week. One reason was that painkillers given during labor lingered in the body, leaving new mothers drowsy and confused.

Because visiting hours were strictly limited, many mothers felt isolated from friends and family. It would have been unthinkable for anyone other than medical staff to be present during birth.

The lying-in hospital Mrs. George sought was a two-story brick building that took up half a city block. In accordance with instructions received from Polly, Mrs. George drove past the entrance and made a left onto a side street, then a second left into an alley. There she parked in front of a delivery van and waited a few moments until a stout gray-haired woman dressed in a nurse's uniform emerged from a back entrance and looked around.

Mrs. George took a clipboard with a typed page on it from the passenger seat and alighted from the car. Without introducing herself, she said, "You must be Polly's acquaintance."

"I am Mrs. Babst." The woman eyed Mrs. George up and down. "Now, about the money…"

"Polly will see to that. I'm sure she explained?" Mrs. George's smile was icy and serene.

Mrs. Babst hesitated, but only for a moment. "Follow me."

This particular hospital, which served the poor of the city, was busy and not especially clean. Gray-brown streaks dappled the walls and speckled the dingy linoleum floor.

Once their babies were born, new mothers were taken to a room with as many as a dozen beds. The babies, in turn, went to the hospital nursery, to be brought to their mothers four times a day for feeding. Those who cried were given only a pacifier, with the result that the baby nursery was a noisy place.

Besides alerting Polly to the birth of a desirable baby, Mrs. Babst was being paid to see to it that his mother had a private room.

The two women passed several nurses and orderlies in the hallway, all of them too harried to pay any attention. Finally, Mrs. Babst stopped in front of an open door and said to Mrs. George, "She's in here." Then she stepped inside. "Mrs. Dimitri?"

In fact, "Mrs." Dimitri had never been married, a shameful

situation for a mother at that time. For propriety's sake, the staff called all the mothers "Mrs."

Mrs. Dimitri was pale, with sunken dark eyes and uncombed hair. The shoulder of her green hospital gown was pulled down so she could nurse her baby, a flannel-blanketed bundle held securely to her chest.

Mrs. George had seen enough new mothers to know that this one's exhausted appearance was normal. In fact, she was relieved to see that the girl looked healthy, with no sign on her cheeks of the spots that could indicate tuberculosis. Her good health boded well for the baby's, a satisfaction to Mrs. George, who preferred not to purvey damaged goods, especially to a buyer as important as Miss Grahame.

"This is the lady I told you about," said Mrs. Babst to Mrs. Dimitri.

"Oh. Yes?" Mrs. Dimitri's puzzled expression said she didn't remember being told about a lady.

"Yes," Mrs. Babst assented. "You just go along and do what she says, now. I have to see to other patients."

Mrs. Babst left without looking back. Mrs. George approached the bed.

"Hello, dear. How are you feeling?" Mrs. George had perfected a brisk, soft-spoken way of addressing new mothers.

"Tired, but they tell me it's normal. Are you a nurse?"

Mrs. George studied the girl, who looked young enough to be in school. "Of course. And I just need your handsome blond boy for a few tests. They won't take long."

The baby was nursing and was held tight in his mother's arms. At first Mrs. George couldn't see his face and had to trust that Polly's friend hadn't let her down, that this was an unblemished, straight-limbed infant good-looking enough to satisfy a movie star.

"He is my handsome boy," Mrs. Dimitri said. "And I'm going to raise him right. That's the important thing, isn't it, Nurse?"

"Certainly it is. Now, I just need your signature on this document. It says you give permission for the tests."

Instead of reaching for the pen, Mrs. Dimitri closed her eyes and lay back against the pillows. "All right. Just let me think a minute. It's all been so much, and I'm so tired."

"I understand, dear," said Mrs. George. "But this is easy. Open your eyes, and I'll show you where to sign. You can write your name, can't you?"

"What kind of tests?" Mrs. Dimitri's eyes remained closed.

"Routine procedures. They won't hurt. The city requires it."

"No needles?" Mrs. Dimitri said.

Mrs. George became aware of time passing. At any moment, some meddlesome doctor or clerk might come in and ask to see the papers in her hand. "Nothing like that," she said. "But I am on a schedule, Mrs. Dimitri. The sooner I take him, the sooner I can bring him back."

Mrs. Dimitri sighed, sat up, rearranged her hospital gown. "All right. Show me again what this is."

The page on the clipboard was typewritten on heavy legal stock. Mrs. Dimitri's full name had already been entered by Judge Mewhinney's clerk, as had the date. All the young mother had to do was sign on the appropriate line. In fact, the wording had nothing to do with medical procedures. Rather, by signing it, Janet Rose Dimitri agreed to give up all parental rights to her newborn son and, under the laws of the City and County of Philadelphia, thereby release him for adoption.

For Mrs. George, this was the moment of truth. Should the girl actually read the documents, she might refuse to sign, might even call out and make a scene. In that case, Mrs. George was prepared to apologize, say she'd made a mistake, and beat a hasty retreat. She had never had to do that before...but she was ready.

Mrs. George felt her heart bump, but her voice was soothing. "Go ahead, dear."

At last, Mrs. Dimitri took the pen, wrote her name in neat, round cursive, handed back the clipboard, and subsided into the pillows.

Seeing the signature, Mrs. George smiled a genuine smile. "I'll just take him, then." She reached down, slid her soft, manicured hands beneath the warm bundle, and lifted.

Well fed and comfortable, the baby boy nestled into her shoulder.

"Good-bye, dear. And thank you," said Mrs. George; then, in three quick strides, she was safe in the hallway.

"Nurse?" Mrs. Dimitri called after her. "Nurse?"

But it was too late. Looking straight ahead, the baby thief strode briskly toward the exit to the alley where her car was waiting.

Chapter Twenty-Five

Caro couldn't imagine why Mrs. George had called her into her office that afternoon. She was sure she hadn't done anything wrong. But Mrs. George was not in the habit of inviting children to her office to praise them.

Halfway down the corridor she figured it out, or thought she did. It was because she had rescued that mouse the other night. Had to be. Caro hadn't smiled since Miss Grahame's visit, but she did now—even if she was about to get in trouble. The mouse had been so dear, seemingly so grateful and polite. Caro knew how Mrs. George hated mice, and rescuing this one was the closest she had ever come to an act of rebellion.

As for the delayed consequences, maybe Matron Polly hadn't told Mrs. George till now?

Caro knew she owed Mrs. George everything. Without her, Caro would have been sent to some terrible place after her mother died. Grateful, Caro had repaid Mrs. George as best she could, doing small things, like wiping the jam off Annabelle's nose, but also more important ones—like setting a good example at chores and at school.

This bargain between them was never spelled out, but Caro thought it created a bond. Not that Caro loved

Mrs. George, exactly. Mrs. George wasn't soft the way a person you loved would be. She was strong and independent instead. And she was one more thing, an important thing. She was good.

Caro knew that. Everybody knew that. There were plaques all over Mrs. George's office wall attesting to it, and photos of her with important people like the president's wife, Mrs. Truman, and the governor's wife, Mrs. Duff. There were cricles from newspapers and magazines articles by the dozen.

Once in a while, however, even good Mrs. George lost her temper—like that time when she boxed Jimmy's ears.

This was on Caro's mind as she knocked on the office door.

"Come in," said Mrs. George.

Caro opened the door, noticing as she did that the headmistress's expression was mild, even sympathetic. So it wasn't the mouse, then. But what?

"Sit down, Carolyn," Mrs. George said. "I just wanted to tell you how sorry I am about the remark Miss Grahame made. It was thoughtless. I'm sure she did not intend to hurt your feelings."

Caro was so taken aback she didn't reply right away. Finally, she said, "No, ma'am," then, "Is that all, ma'am?"

"No." Mrs. George rose from her chair. "Come with me. I have a little job for you to do."

Baffled, Caro followed Mrs. George up the stairs to the second floor and down the hallway past the classrooms. When at last they turned into the nursery, Caro saw that one of the bassinettes was occupied.

"Oh!" she gasped, and ran to look. "It's a tiny one! Boy or girl?"

"Boy," said Mrs. George.

Caro studied the baby, who looked toward her with deep-blue unfocused eyes. His face was red and scrunched under a fuzzy thatch of pale hair. On the side of his head, just above the ears, were pale purple bruises. Caro knew what that meant. The doctor had used a forceps to help with delivery, and the forceps had left the marks.

Bruises and all, the boy was beautiful. "Why is he here at Cherry Street?" Caro asked.

Mrs. George pursed her lips. "A terrible thing. The police found him abandoned on the doorstep of one of the precinct houses. Not even a note. He's lucky a stray dog didn't take him."

Caro shuddered, but she was not shocked. The children at Cherry Street knew bad things happened in the world. Some of the children had suffered very bad things themselves, or seen other children suffer, and they talked about it. How could they not?

"But now he's safe," said Mrs. George briskly, "and just awakened from his nap. Matron Polly has changed his diaper, powdered him, and given him formula in a bottle. He'll be fed again at five p.m."

"You mean I'm to take care of him till then?"

Among the items in the cupboard the Cherry Street Home provided for Caro's possessions was a baby doll given by church ladies four Christmases ago. She didn't play with it anymore. She couldn't without being teased. But every time she opened her cupboard and saw it, she thought of how it would have been to have a baby sister or brother—a family of her own.

Now, at least for a little while, she'd have a baby to herself, something wriggly and warm and special, just for Caro.

"Matron Polly will assist if you need her," said Mrs. George. "Keep him comfortable. Carry him if he's fussy. Lay him down in his crib if he's not. Young ones like this sleep most of the time."

"May I show him to the other girls?" Caro asked.

"Yes, provided they don't have colds and they wash their hands," said Mrs. George. "You don't have a cold, do you?"

"No, ma'am," said Caro. "What's his name?"

"He doesn't have one," said Mrs. George. "The birth certificate, when the clerk prepares it, will just say 'Baby Boy,' the date he was found, and the location."

"May I name him?" Caro asked.

"For the afternoon, I suppose you may."

A few minutes later, Caro walked into the main parlor with a baby in her arms . . . and caused a commotion.

"Can I hold him?" "Lucky—I want a baby to play with!" "What's his name?"

"Charlie." Caro had named him after her war hero father. "And you may hold him once you've washed your hands."

The three intermediate girls went to the washroom and returned, still clamoring to hold the baby.

"Can I feed him?" Barbara took Charlie.

"No, me!" said Virginia.

"Ew—I think he's stinky," said Betty.

"He is not," said Caro.

"What are those marks on his head? They look like ink spots," Barbara said.

"It's from when he was born," Virginia explained. "If there's trouble and the baby gets stuck, the doctor uses an instrument called forceps. Sometimes they leave a mark."

Caro already knew this and had stopped listening to her friends. Instead, she was thinking. The use of forceps meant Charlie had been delivered in a hospital. Delivered in a hospital...then abandoned at a police station? It didn't make sense. Was Mrs. George mistaken?

The drowsy infant was passed from girl to girl under the watchful eye of Matron Polly, who did not interfere because she believed a quiet baby was a happy baby. Charlie himself dozed most of the time and made funny faces when he was awake. His best trick, the girls agreed, was yawning.

While Caro found Charlie endlessly fascinating, the other girls eventually grew bored. When he started to cry—a shrill, breathy, birdlike sound—they went looking for other things to do. Caro found Matron Polly in the kitchen helping Mrs. Spinelli with dinner. Matron Polly looked at her watch. "Another forty-five minutes yet."

"But he's hungry now," Caro said.

Polly shrugged. "That can't be helped. If he doesn't have a schedule, he'll become a little tyrant."

Caro knew hunger made your stomach hurt, and she couldn't bear the idea of that for Charlie. What did a tiny baby know about schedules?

Caro argued, but Matron Polly only shrugged. "I didn't make the world."

To console him, Caro held the baby against her shoulder, went up the stairs, and walked in and out of the empty classrooms, narrating all that she saw: "This is the American flag,

this is a map of Pennsylvania, these white things are called chalk, these are books, these are the letters of the alphabet..."

Baby Charlie listened for a while, whimpered, wailed, and settled down again. Finally, it was five o'clock, and Caro returned to the nursery, where Matron Polly placed a bottle in a silver contraption that warmed formula to precise body temperature.

Caro handed Charlie over reluctantly.

"Can I take care of him again tomorrow?" she asked.

Matron Polly shrugged. "I don't see why not."

Chapter Twenty-Six

There had never been a Mr. George.

At twenty-one, the age when most women of her era married, pretty Helen George had had her share of suitors. But she didn't care much for any of them, and certainly had no intention of sharing her life with one. Having grown up in Pennsylvania coal country with too large a family and too little money, Helen believed she had had quite enough of sharing for one lifetime.

But this was 1925, and a single woman—a spinster—was seen as pitiable or suspect. Something must be wrong. Normal girls married. So when she left home for the big city of Philadelphia, Helen invented a handsome young husband, named him Douglas after her favorite film star, then killed him off with a rare, unpronounceable disease.

Voilà! In the eyes of the world, Helen George was now a respectable young widow.

In Philadelphia, Mrs. George studied bookkeeping at a secretarial school, worked hard, and lived frugally in a rooming house where one of the other lodgers introduced her to a small-time bootlegger who was better at selling illegal rum than keeping track of profits.

The 1920s were the era of Prohibition, when the government made alcohol illegal to prevent people from drinking. Like a lot of good ideas, it didn't work. People continued to drink, but now they bought their beer, wine, and liquor from enterprising criminals who smuggled it from abroad or made it themselves.

If Helen George had any qualms about involving herself with crime, she got over them when she saw how much money she was making. All her life she had scrimped and saved. All her life she had been poor. Now the steadily increasing sums in her bankbook told her those days were over. She finished school, bought a small house and more fashionable clothes, then found a daytime job in a lawyer's office—all while continuing to keep books for the bootlegger. By the time Prohibition ended in 1933, he had expanded operations to the point that he was a significant force in the Philadelphia underworld.

Too significant, it turned out.

In the spring of 1934, he was shot dead in front of a South Seventh Street restaurant. Truthfully, Mrs. George wasn't surprised...and by this time she wasn't sorry, either. The business had become risky. She did not want to go to jail. She had been looking for a way to preserve her liberty, her skin, her tidy nest egg, and her improved social status—all without making her friend the onetime bootlegger mad.

Making him mad, as all his associates well knew, could be a bruising experience.

Anyway, now her problem was solved.

Helen continued to work for the law office until, a year later, one of the lawyers mentioned her to his friend Philips-Bodbetter. At their initial interview, Mrs. George suppressed a smile when asked if she had previous experience working with children. Oh, yes. Plenty. Hadn't she run a household with five younger siblings from the time she was ten years old? A household where the only source of income was her mama's paltry wages from cleaning for those better off?

But that was not the kind of experience these people wanted to hear about. They wanted her to have been a teacher at a school for girls, something in that line. So Mrs. George lied with her usual smoothness. Why, yes, she had indeed. Before marrying the late lamented Douglas George, she had taught school in her hometown. As for references, she would be happy to provide the name of the superintendent, only she couldn't be sure the address was still accurate. It had been more than a decade, after all.

Chapter Twenty-Seven

When Judge Mewhinney was anxious or upset, he blinked in a rapid, twitchy way that about drove Helen George crazy.

"My dear," she said gently, "could you stop that? Please?"

It was Wednesday evening, and the two were drinking sherry in her parlor, the judge sitting in the club chair, his cigar in an ashtray by his side, she on the chintz sofa across the room.

The two were arguing, Mrs. George struggling to keep her temper in check.

Hadn't her part of the operation gone perfectly?

Didn't she deserve some credit?

Instead, the judge seemed to take for granted her success—easy to do, she supposed, when his own part of the business consisted of signing papers in the comfort of his office. Adding insult to injury, he now dared to question whether their business records were safe in her keeping.

"Stop what?" he asked—blink-blink-blink.

Mrs. George sighed. "Never mind." It would be simpler if she just looked away.

"I have a locked safe in my office in the courthouse, which is well protected by police," said the judge. "Your so-called hiding place can't possibly be as secure."

"It is because it's secret," she said. "In contrast to the courthouse, no one ever visits this apartment except Polly in the afternoons, and you in the evenings. Now"—she tried to change the subject—"I believe you have a document for me? And I have one for you."

Mrs. George disturbed the napping cat when she rose to retrieve the papers from the writing desk by the door. The judge, meanwhile, took a puff of his cigar before pulling his briefcase into his lap, removing a sheet of paper, and reading aloud:

"'Certificate of a live birth in the City and County of Philadelphia. Sex: male. Race: Caucasian. Mother: Janet Rose Dimitri. Father…' Hmmm." The judge looked up. "That has been left blank. 'Birth weight and length:' Et cetera. Et cetera. In short, we have a healthy baby boy. 'Name: Arthur Robert Dimitri.'"

"Not anymore." Mrs. George handed the judge the adoption papers Mrs. Dimitri had signed. "In fact, Carolyn renamed him Charlie this afternoon, according to Polly. And Miss Grahame will have her own name for him, his real name."

The judge put the adoption release into his briefcase, which he then closed and latched.

"You'll file that with the clerk tomorrow?" Mrs. George said.

"And the clerk will issue the amended birth certificate, making it all but impossible for Miss Dimitri to find her son—if ever she were inclined to do so."

"He's no longer her son," said Mrs. George. "He's a lucky little boy who's getting—"

"—an opportunity he never could have expected." The judge finished her sentence. "Yes, I know, Helen. And Miss Grahame gets the blond baby she's always wanted, and we get—"

"—an appropriate fee." Mrs. George interrupted in case he was about to say something as vulgar as "rich" or "money" or "cash."

"What about Miss Dimitri?" the judge asked, blink-blink-blink. "What does she get?"

Mrs. George was running out of patience. "Miss Dimitri has only herself to blame for getting into trouble. We've been through all this before, Jonathan."

On the lamp table by the love seat was a manila folder labeled *Joanna Grahame*. Mrs. George slipped the birth certificate inside and laid it back on the table. Then she sat down, picked up her glass, and sipped her sherry.

After a few moments, the judge asked, "When does the boy go to his new home?"

"Miss Grahame has obtained a nurse through an agency. The nurse is traveling here by automobile. She will stay the night in a hotel and come here before breakfast tomorrow. Once she has the boy, she'll return with him to New York City, and there he'll be united with his mother. Miss Grahame and her son go home to California next week."

"There to live happily ever after," said the judge.

Mrs. George said tartly that she had no reason to expect otherwise. Then, pleading a headache, she announced she would turn in early. The judge left shortly after that...but Mrs. George did not retire immediately to her bedroom. Instead, she stood quietly in her parlor, listening as her caller's footfalls grew fainter on the stairs. When she could no longer hear them, she took Joanna Grahame's folder from the lamp table, went into the kitchen, wrapped it snugly in white butcher paper, and secreted it in a hiding place whose location even the judge did not know.

Chapter Twenty-Eight

———⊰•⊱———

For a legend, Andrew Mouse was awfully annoying.

That was Mary Mouse's assessment, and they hadn't even been together a full twenty-four hours.

He followed her around. He never shut up. If she had an idea, he had one, too. To his credit, he was willing to apologize. But that turned out to be a mixed blessing when his apologies went on so long they became monologues in a one-mouse show:

"Do I talk too much? I talk too much. I'm sorry I talk so much. I don't mean to. It's just that I was alone so long. It's like I stored up all these words and now they're spilling out. Tell me I don't talk too much. But I do. Don't I?"

"Yes," Mary said.

"Ha ha ha ha ha!" said Andrew, and then he asked, "Have I told you the story of why I went away?"

It was midday for the mice, the middle of the night in human time. On their spy mission earlier, Mary and Andrew had inhaled more cigar smoke than was good for them, and gained two pieces of intelligence. First, the boss had obtained the new human pup in the nursery by thievery. Second, her hiding place for papers was the cold white box in the kitchen of her apartment, the box that otherwise held comestibles.

Andrew and Mary were both professional thieves, but neither had heard of stealing a pup, let alone stealing a pup to trade. Mary had been horrified, Andrew somewhat less so. Human behavior, he reminded her, was infinitely strange.

At any rate, neither of these pieces of intelligence pertained to them. The important thing was that no one had mentioned an exterminator, and, in other news, the predator had not ventured from the sofa.

Now Mary looked forward to lunch in a pleasant cellar picnic spot where a grate high in the cinder-block wall afforded a breeze.

"No, Andrew," Mary said in response to his question. "You haven't told me yet why you left, but I have a feeling you're about to."

Andrew's whiskers drooped. "I won't if you don't want me to. I suppose it's not very interesting. I suppose *I'm* not very interesting. I'm boring, aren't I? I'm sorry."

Mary sighed. "Go ahead and tell me." While he talked, she calculated, she could finish the last of the tomato seeds they'd foraged for their meal.

"You see"—Andrew brightened—"I wanted to be like Stuart Little himself. He left his family—"

"—his parents, Mr. and Mrs. Frederick C. Little, and his brother George, of New York City," Mary recited.

"—and borrowed a sports car from his friend the surgeon dentist, and drove out of the city in search of Margalo—"

"—the pretty little brown hen-bird with a streak of yellow on her breast."

"Precisely," said Andrew.

"Did you have a car?" Mary asked.

The idea of a car had been fascinating and attractive to the mice of the Cherry Street colony. Scurrying could only get you so far.

"Sadly, no," Andrew said. "I hitched a ride on a newspaper delivery truck, which is how I ended up at the Market Street Newsstand." He tried to say this modestly, but the sparkle in his eye gave away his pride. Leaping from the sidewalk to the truck's running board had been no mean feat.

"And was there a Margalo?" Mary asked.

Andrew said, "If you truly wish to understand my story, Mary Mouse, I will have to begin at the beginning."

Chapter Twenty-Nine

Andrew arranged his tail, settled back on his haunches, clasped his front paws one in the other, and began: "I was a puny pup."

Oh, dear, thought Mary. *We really are going back to the beginning.*

"And furthermore," Andrew continued, "I was picked on by my brothers and sisters, my cousins, even my uncle Fitzgerald. Another mouse might have been defeated by such harsh treatment, but I determined to overcome it, to make something of myself.

"How did I do this? First, I set a schedule and did pull-ups, push-ups, and tail-ups every day. In addition, I ate only healthy scraps. I meant to avoid growing plump..."

Mary vowed to eat only one more tomato seed, two at most.

"...so that I could squeeze in and out of the tiniest spaces and, with my superior speed and agility, elude all predators."

Mary swallowed. "What about mental training?"

Andrew looked up as if he was surprised to be interrupted. "Ah, of course. Well, more than any mouse excepting the scholars, I studied the story of Stuart Little. And the more I learned, the more I realized that I must follow in his mouse-tracks if I wanted to attain wisdom."

"And did you attain wisdom?"

A little exasperated, Andrew said, "That came later."

"Sorry," Mary said.

Andrew scratched his haunch. "Where was I? Oh, yes. The only way to follow the path of Stuart was to liberate myself from the colony. I had observed that the newspaper delivery truck came to the home on a fixed schedule in the early morning. Knowing I would have only one chance to make my escape, I practiced the necessary maneuvers over and over again, using the running boards of vehicles parked at the curb as targets.

"It was a dark and cold winter morning when at last I made my move. I did not say good-bye. Carrying nothing, I squeezed through the foyer portal, then scurried beneath the front gate. Waiting at the curb, shivering and alone, I soon heard the deep rumble of truck tires on the macadam and saw headlights in the gloom. The brakes squealed. The truck stopped. The driver rolled down his window and tossed a newspaper over the fence.

"I had only a few seconds, and I made the most of them. I leaped to the running board and dug my claws into the rubber."

Mary's heart pounded in sympathy.

"I felt exultant! I thought I was safe," said Andrew.

"And weren't you?" Mary asked.

Andrew shook his head. "I hadn't counted on one thing—the rush of freezing wind that followed the truck's acceleration. It dislodged my claws and pushed me backward toward the precipice. At any second, I expected to be dashed to my death!"

Mary shuddered. This was a good story. Lots of suspense.

"Then, at the last possible moment, the truck braked, and I somersaulted forward. I was dizzy and off-balance, but when the driver's door opened, I managed to stumble sideways into the truck's cab. A few minutes later, the truck stopped to drop off a bundle of newspapers at the Market Street Newsstand, and the driver alighted to visit with the owner, Mr. Valenti. That was when I took the opportunity to disembark."

"Why there?" Mary asked.

Andrew's beady eyes turned dreamy. "It was the smell of people and comestibles," he said. "I was ravenous, and the newsstand smells were delicious. I thought I could do worse than to make it the first stop on my quest."

"But it wasn't the first stop," said Mary. "You stayed there."

Andrew nodded. "I did."

Mary felt a little harrumph of satisfaction. So the big-time, boy-wonder mouse hadn't gone on such a magnificent odyssey at all. He had gone to the Market Street Newsstand...and *finis*. She thought of a question.

"Uh, just what exactly is a newsstand?"

"A wonderful place," Andrew said, "a small wooden shelter that's busy all day with humans learning the news of the world from colorful and interesting magazines and newspapers, some of them with photographs."

"Are there photographs of mice?" Mary asked.

"There is an occasional photograph of"—Andrew lowered his voice to a whisper—"*rats*. And they are always shown in an unfavorable light."

"Naturally," said Mary.

"Besides that, there are photographs of predators and, even more often, of canines. But the vast majority of the photographs show humans."

"Such a self-centered species," said Mary.

"The newsstand was a good home," Andrew said, "but it did have its perils. Mr. Valenti was larger even than the usual full-grown male, and he often wore heavy boots. While usually it was easy to hear him coming, I still worried about being squashed. Also, the newsstand was only open from five-thirty a.m. till eight p.m., which meant there was no heat overnight."

"And you mentioned the comestibles?" Mary prompted.

Andrew offered a detailed and rhapsodic account of the candies, gums, nuts, crackers, and packaged cookies on offer at the Market Street Newsstand, besides well-considered opinions on the merits of Wrigley's spearmint versus Juicy Fruit gum and Milky Way versus Hershey chocolate bars.

"Was it the quality of the comestibles that kept you from leaving the newsstand and completing your quest?"

Andrew's whiskers bristled. "Who says I did not complete my quest? At the Market Street Newsstand, I realized that the true nature of my quest was not spatial but mental."

Mary covered her mouth with her paw to keep from

laughing. Did he not know how pompous he sounded? But when his whiskers drooped again, she felt a pang of remorse. "Please continue," she said.

Andrew wiped his paw across his face. "At the Market Street Newsstand..." he began, then stopped and cocked his head. "Where was I?"

Mary came to a realization. "Andrew Mouse," she said, "have you memorized your story word for word?"

The auditors had memorized the story of Stuart Little word for word, and most mice knew a few passages by heart. But it would be strange for a mouse to memorize a personal story so exactly. The implication was that the story must be very, very important.

Andrew looked sheepish. "Yeah. I practiced a lot."

Mary could just see it. All alone on cold winter nights in the newsstand, Andrew pacing back and forth to keep warm while declaiming the story of his life. Probably he had envisioned his triumphant return to the colony, the crowds of cheering auditors, the tale retold over Cherry Street generations. Instead, the populace had gone away, and his only auditor, Mary Mouse, had not cheered even once.

Andrew's likely disappointment awakened her sympathy. "A mental journey," she prompted.

"Right," he said. "In short, the way that I attained wisdom and fulfillment and completed my quest was this: I learned to read."

Chapter Thirty

Mary was flabbergasted.

For generations, the auditors of the Cherry Street colony had observed that when Miss Ragone told a story, she looked at the book she held and at regular intervals turned its pages. From this observation, they concluded that the markings on the book's pages contained the story, which Miss Ragone deciphered through the process the humans called reading.

Mice had to memorize every story they told. How convenient for human beings that they did not!

The auditors—whose job was to listen to stories, then retell them—were especially eager to learn this useful human trick. From their observations of the classrooms on the second floor, they deduced that Miss Ragone taught the human pups to read, and the auditors duly attended her lessons. In addition, thieves were assigned to steal pages for the auditors to study. But try as they might, the mice could never make sense of the marks on the pages. They did not resemble words, but only misshapen mouse-tracks.

"Please forgive my skepticism," Mary said to Andrew, "but the colony's wisest mice have tried and failed to learn to read. Why were you able to do so on your own?"

"I had certain advantages," Andrew said modestly, "including an almost infinite supply of reading material at the newsstand, and the lack of distractions like a social life, or pups."

Mary felt a pang at the mention of pups. How were her own girls faring? Had they arrived at their new home safely?

"Mary?" Andrew cocked his head. "Are you all right?"

"Yes, of course," she said. "It's just—"

"What a bonehead I am," Andrew said. "You miss your own pups, don't you? I shouldn't have spoken so casually."

Mary wiped her nose and shook out her whiskers. "Tell me how you did it, how you learned to read."

Andrew continued his story. "There was a male human pup who visited the newsstand sometimes," he explained. "His name was Mario, and he was very badly behaved. He tried to steal candy when no one was looking, and comic books, too."

"A thief like us," Mary said.

Andrew disagreed. "Not at all. We stole only for the good of the colony. This little Mario stole out of greed."

Mary conceded the point. "I see."

"Also, he was not very skillful and always got caught," Andrew went on. "But Mr. Valenti, in spite of his heavy boots, was a kind man. When Mario's mama told him Mario was having trouble in school, Mr. Valenti offered to help him with his reading. Since there were no schoolbooks at the newsstand, Mr. Valenti taught him by using newspaper headlines."

"What are newspaper headlines?" Mary asked.

"The words at the top of each newspaper story, the title,"

Andrew explained. "Over and over, Mr. Valenti read Mario the words in the headlines, and Mario repeated them. After a while, I noticed how often the same words appeared—words like *Truman,* who is the chief director of the human territory in which our colony is located; and *Korea,* which is another territory, one that's very far away; and *war*—well, every mouse knows what war is. Because the headlines were simple and the words repeated, I began to recognize some of them. From this, I saw where our auditors had gone wrong."

"Where?" asked Mary.

"All along, the auditors had assumed the marks were pictures. What I realized was that each mark represents a sound, and then the sounds combine to form words. After that, the marks, which are actually called letters, started to make sense."

Mary knew just enough about reading to see how this might be true. "And after that you could read?" she asked.

"Not as well as I thought I could," Andrew said. "The more I studied, the more I realized that reading is more complicated than just knowing each letter's sounds. Sometimes there are tricks and a letter makes no sound at all. Sometimes letters represent one sound in one word, and a different sound in the next. Take *o,u,g,h,* for example. It might be *ooh,* as in *through,* or *oh,* as in *thorough,* or *aw,* as in *ought,* or *uff,* as in *rough* and *tough.*"

Mary nodded...even though he had lost her completely.

"Also," Andrew went on, "when you think about it, why

is there a *g* in there at all? If reading English made any sense, *o,u,g,h* would be pronounced *owg*, and yet it never is."

Thoroughly confused, Mary nodded again. "How very true. But"—she hoped she was not asking too big a favor—"can you show me?"

Andrew seemed gratified to be asked. "I will," he said, "just as soon as the newspaper arrives in the morning. Does the boss still keep it in her office?"

Mary nodded. "Jimmy brings it in and puts it on her desk. But it's too heavy for us to steal, and the boss would certainly notice it was gone."

"We don't need all of it, only a small piece," said Andrew. "Trust me, the boss will never notice it's gone."

Chapter Thirty-One

———◆———

Shortly after sunrise, Mary and Andrew watched from behind the crack in the baseboard as Jimmy laid the newspaper on the boss's desk. When he left, they scurried across the oak floor and the deep-piled rug before making the climb up the steep face to the plateau above. As thieves of the colony, both were thoroughly familiar with the desktop and its landmarks. For her part, Mary couldn't help thinking how much her life had changed since the last time she'd been there.

This was no time for reflection. There was hardly time for a deep breath. By Mary's calculations, they had only about a quarter hour to carry out their mission.

In the hours before morning, the two thieves had planned each maneuver and practiced. Now, without so much as a squeak, they bit down on opposite corners of the front page, then pulled and yanked till the newspaper had unfolded and lay flat.

Next came the hard part, flipping the entire paper over.

This was because—according to Andrew—the back page was less important than the front. Thus it would be even less obvious to the boss if the missing square came from the back.

Working together, Mary and Andrew bit the right top

corner and scooted backward diagonally, pulling the corner with them. By this time, Mary had regained full strength in her wounded shoulder still the work was exhausting. At last she felt the weight of the paper shift, and...they had done it! The back page was on top.

Now it was up to Andrew to choose the square he wanted, so Mary sat back as he studied the markings. Was he really reading? She would soon know. When he pointed his nose at a spot near the page's edge, Mary went to work.

Nothing gnaws like a mouse, and soon the square Andrew wanted was detached. Flipping the newspaper was easier the second time; then Andrew took a moment to align it with the edge of the desk. There was, unfortunately, no way for the mice to refold it in two. They would just have to hope the boss had other things on her mind.

With her nose, Mary pushed the square off the edge of the desk. Once it had floated safely to the rug, Andrew leaped from the desk—the show-off—and Mary slid down the cord attached to the black talking box. To carry the paper back to the portal, the two mice balanced it across both their backs, bent their tails over the top to keep it in place, and ran across the room, their noses side by side.

By now the sun was well up, and they could hear Mrs. Spinelli's footfalls in the kitchen. They had worked efficiently. There should be time enough to complete the mission as planned.

Beginning to breathe easier, Mary squeezed through the

portal and waited in mouse territory for Andrew to slide a corner of the paper under the baseboard. When it appeared, she gripped it in her teeth and tugged, but then—*oh, no!* Were those the footfalls of the boss in the corridor? What was she doing downstairs so early?

Andrew must have heard the sound as well, because he squeezed through the narrow portal, gripped an edge of the paper between his teeth, and—alongside Mary—pulled with all his might. The paper had to be safely hidden before the boss entered. Should she see it sliding under the baseboard, whom could she blame but mice?

Yank-yank-yank, and...success!

Just in time, too. The creak of the hinge told the mice the boss was in her office. Mary sat back on her haunches, closed her eyes, and heaved a sigh of relief. When she opened her eyes, she saw that Andrew was smiling at her.

Chapter Thirty-Two

Andrew Mouse was smitten with Mary. She was not only attractive and accomplished, she was so conveniently available. If only she had been smitten with him, too, but alas, she'd made it obvious she was not.

Reading was his chance to impress her, a chance he did not want to lose.

"I need to see clearly to read aloud," he said when at last they had the paper laid out before them. "Is there a place with better light?"

Mary thought for a moment. "I believe there is a spot quite near the directorate where the daylight shines through a chink in the mortar. Will that do?"

Andrew nodded. "We can roll up the paper to carry it. But do you want to sleep first? It's awfully late, and we've been up for hours."

"I'm much too excited to sleep," Mary said. "To think, I am going to witness a mouse *reading*!"

Mary's enthusiasm made Andrew nervous. What if he disappointed her? What if he stammered? He didn't think he could bear it if she laughed.

Using their paws and noses, the two mice rolled the paper

into a neat cylinder and set out. The journey to the nursery required a climb up the plumbing and a trek the full length of the second-floor corridor. Andrew found it awkward traveling in a confined space with a roll of paper between his teeth. Finally—after almost half an hour—the two arrived at the well-lit location that Mary had remembered.

"Will this do?" Mary asked.

Andrew assessed the spotlight of sun on the dusty floor-boards. "Admirably," he said.

Together, the two mice unrolled the paper, now frayed and dirty, and Andrew studied the print before him.

"Well?" Mary said impatiently. "What does it say?"

Andrew knew exactly what it said but prolonged the suspense to make a greater impression. Finally, he harrumphed a couple of times, straightened his ears, and—indicating each word with the tip of his tail—spoke in a resounding squeak: "'Baby Boy Taken.'"

Chapter Thirty-Three

When Caro awoke Thursday morning, she had all but forgotten Miss Grahame's insult. In fact, she was happier than she had been in a very long time. In her mind's eye was the face of a tiny baby: Charlie!

But when she asked Matron Polly about him at breakfast, she got a rude surprise.

"You won't be taking care of him today after all," said Matron.

Caro felt as if she'd been slapped. "Why not?"

Matron did not look her in the eye. "Because you can't," she said.

Feeling her stomach twist, Caro pushed her oatmeal away and asked to be excused. Then, instead of returning to the intermediate girls' dormitory, she continued down the corridor beyond it to the baby nursery. As she approached, she could tell that something was wrong. It was dead quiet, and the nursery door was closed. She opened it a crack, peeked inside, then pushed the door wide.

The bassinette was empty.

At first, Caro tried to reassure herself. Maybe Mr. Donald or Mrs. George had simply taken Charlie outdoors for fresh air?

But then she noticed something else. The diaper pail was missing and the changing table, which had been stocked with diapers and a few tiny T-shirts, was bare.

Involuntarily, Caro cried out.

Charlie was gone.

Chapter Thirty-Four

———◆———

Andrew had been almost done with the story when he was interrupted by a human cry from the nursery. It was a single, guttural note of anguish—terrible to hear, even if you didn't yourself happen to be human.

"My stars—which one is that?" he asked Mary.

Mary knew her rescuer's voice. "Caro," she said. "Come on."

The two mice trotted north a few mousetails to an unused electrical socket. Through its slots they could see Caro staring into the bassinette.

"The newborn pup is missing," Mary said. "Andrew—is it possible that pup is the same one from the story you've been reading to me?"

This had also occurred to Andrew, but he played dumb in the interests of improving relations with Mary. "What an idea!" he said. "And how very clever of you to come up with it."

Upset by Caro's distress, Mary did not even note the compliment.

Chapter Thirty-Five

Caro's head swam, and she reached for the crib railing to steady herself. The sudden heartbreak over Charlie's disappearance recalled an earlier catastrophe, and sensations from the night her mother died intruded with hallucinatory intensity: her hand and arm burned; she could swear she heard screaming.

Caro closed her eyes and was overwhelmed: Smoke, heat, light. Searing pain in her lungs. A poisonous taste in her mouth. Beyond that—a blur. What she knew about that night was what she had been told: She had ignored her mother's cries and saved herself. She had run. She had burned her hand on the searing-hot metal of the doorknob as she twisted it to free herself, to escape. She had failed her mother, the only person in the world who loved her. She was a coward.

Caro had lived with this guilt for five years. And for five years she had tried to atone by being perfect.

But now she had failed again, failed to save Charlie. She remembered the inconsistency between forceps marks and abandonment on the doorstep of a police station. Something did not make sense.

"Oh, there you are." Matron Polly's voice made her jump. "Mrs. George said you'd be here."

"What happened to Charlie?" Caro's voice rasped.

"Why, Caro, child, what's the matter?" Polly asked. "You're crying!"

Caro wiped her face with the back of her hand, sniffed back her tears. "Where's Charlie?"

"Now, now. Mrs. George is wanting to tell you all about that. She's in her office."

Chapter Thirty-Six

—————◆—————

Mrs. George was on the telephone when Matron Polly brought Carolyn into her office. By this time, the headmistress had already been at work for several hours, her day having begun before breakfast when she met Miss Grahame's baby nurse in the foyer. With Polly's help, she had transferred the infant boy; his few blankets, T-shirts, and diapers; and the official birth and adoption documents provided by Judge Mewhinney.

In exchange, the nurse had given Mrs. George a sealed envelope of gratifying heft. If Joanna Grahame wondered why Mrs. George asked for cash instead of a personal check, she didn't mention it. Perhaps she knew that in certain matters of a confidential nature, cash—being more difficult to trace—was preferable.

Now, still on the telephone, Mrs. George gestured for Polly and Carolyn to come in.

"A week from Monday simply won't do," she told the secretary at the exterminating service.

"Well, that's our first opening," the woman replied.

"I'm sure Mr. Philips-Bodbetter would appreciate it if you could alter your schedule," said Mrs. George.

"Mr. Philips-Bodbetter?" The secretary was obviously

impressed. "Well, in that case...Please wait one minute.... Perhaps this Saturday?"

"Saturday morning is fine," said Mrs. George. "Nine o'clock."

Without saying good-bye, she returned the receiver to its cradle.

Polly did not mask her dismay. "The exterminator's coming Saturday? But that hardly gives us time to make arrangements for the children."

Mrs. George held up a torn scrap of paper. "I found this on the floor clear across the room." She indicated a spot by the baseboard. "And would you look at this?" She held up her newspaper, which had a hole in the back.

Polly frowned. "What would mice want with newspaper, ma'am?"

"I'm sure I don't know what mice want," said Mrs. George, "but their vile little tooth-marks are everywhere. So, while I apologize for the short notice, it can't be helped. Now"—she sat down and smoothed her hair—"while you see that the girls are getting on with their chores, Carolyn and I will have a little chat."

Polly said, "Yes, ma'am," but Mrs. George could see by the woman's squint—more pronounced than usual—and by her heightened color that she was unhappy. Would she make trouble? She never had before, and she was well compensated for her services. Mrs. George even kept bottles of beer for her in the refrigerator of her private apartment, allowed her to take her break from the children there each afternoon. Surely her generosity would count for something.

And Polly didn't like mice any more than Mrs. George did.

"Sit down, dear," Mrs. George said to Carolyn after the matron had left. "I'm sorry there was no chance for you to say good-bye to the infant. What was it you called him? Charlie?"

"It was my father's name," said Carolyn.

Mrs. George felt a pang that surprised her. Surely, she wasn't thinking of her own father? "Ah. Well, this little boy has been adopted by a very fine mother…that is, family. And now he will have every advantage. He's quite lucky."

"But where is he?" Carolyn asked. "And why did he have to leave so quickly?"

It wasn't like Carolyn to ask difficult questions. "You've been here long enough to know how it is in matters of adoption, Carolyn," said Mrs. George. "I can't give out any information, not even to you. Some people blame an orphan for his unlucky origins, and we would never want any of our children to carry that shame."

Carolyn persisted. "Mrs. George," she asked, "who brought Charlie to the home?"

Mrs. George opened the top drawer of her desk to signal that their interview was over. "The police did, dear. I already explained. Now, I'm sure Matron Polly needs—"

"Because something's confusing me," Carolyn went on. "Charlie had marks from a forceps on his head. I know that's what the marks were. I've seen them before."

Mrs. George closed her desk drawer but didn't look up. *Oh, dear.*

"And you said," Carolyn continued, "that he was abandoned at the police station. But I don't see how that can be if he was delivered with forceps by a doctor. Mothers who deliver in hospitals don't abandon their babies. There's a record of the birth, so they'd be caught. The only mothers who drop off their babies that way are ones who deliver babies by themselves at home, or . . . or someplace else."

Mrs. George's thoughts were racing, but she spoke slowly. "For a child your age, you know quite a lot about a very delicate subject."

"We all do, ma'am," Carolyn said. "I'm sorry if it's not right for children to know, but we can't help it."

Mrs. George sighed. "I suppose not. Well, in this case, perhaps there was some mistake in the story the police officer told me."

"That must be it," Carolyn said thoughtfully, but she did not sound convinced. "Did you talk to Mr. Kittaning?"

"Not necessary," said Mrs. George.

"Because he might know more about where—" Carolyn continued, but Mrs. George had had enough.

"Carolyn!" She spoke more sharply than she intended. "The infant is gone. Your speculation is not helpful. Now, please. I have work to do."

Chapter Thirty-Seven

Andrew and Mary had left the second floor for the boss's office at the same time Matron Polly and Caro did, but their route was longer and their legs shorter. By the time they arrived at the baseboard portal, Matron Polly was leaving.

Rapt, the two mice watched the boss and Caro conversing. They did not understand everything. But they saw that Caro, Mary's rescuer, was upset and suspicious about the newborn pup's disappearance. And they saw that the boss was angry and disdainful.

"I think the boss is hateful!" Mary told Andrew after Caro had been dismissed.

"She is," said Andrew.

"We need to tell Caro what we know," said Mary.

"Do we?" Andrew was surprised.

Mary sat back on her haunches. "I know Caro's merely human, but I feel the need to help her. I'm not sure why. Because my pups are gone? Because I can't do anything for them anymore?"

Andrew spoke gently. "But humans despise us, Mary. If we mice start helping them, where will it lead? Will we soon be helping predators?"

Mary didn't answer right away, and Andrew thought she had seen reason. Then she asked, "Have you ever seen the blue lady?"

Oh dear, thought Andrew. *Perhaps the stress has caused mental unbalance. Better to humor her.*

"O'Brien's picture?" he answered carefully. "Yes, there is a copy in the chief director's collection."

Mary turned, then looked back over her shoulder. "Are you coming?"

The main body of Andrew's collection was housed in an annex of his nest that could only be reached through a length of abandoned sewer pipe. Like the boss's office it was on the shelter's ground floor. By now, the two mice had been awake many hours past their bedtime, but Mary kept up a brisk place, and soon they were descending through the pipe.

Both Mary and Andrew had viewed the chief director's collection before. Still, when they emerged from the pipe's dark confines into the grand expanse, they were dazzled anew by the sight. So many pictures! So much color! All this beauty in one place was more than any mouse could absorb.

There were many portraits among the pictures. Prized for its historic significance, O'Brien's blue lady was displayed by itself on a clean sheet of corrugated cardboard.

"She's not bad-looking for a human," said Andrew as he regarded her.

"Does that writing spell out her name?" Mary used the tip of her tail to indicate the letters.

"'Louisa May Alcott,'" Andrew read. "I wonder who she was."

"*That's it!*" Mary squeaked so loudly that Andrew had to step back and rub his ears. "*Wonder* is precisely the point. Do you see?"

"Uh...no," said Andrew.

Mary sighed. "It's hard to explain, but I will try. Here in our actual lives, we mice can only ever see so much. But pictures enlarge the view, reveal the possibility of worlds we never suspected. Even the pictures that aren't beautiful make us curious, they make us *wonder*."

"Are you with me so far?"

Andrew scratched his ear. "I guess."

"And when Caro asked me about being a mouse," Mary went on, "she did the same thing. She *wondered*."

"Ah," said Andrew, still puzzled but trying gamely to penetrate the mysteries of this female's mind. "So you're saying, if I understand you correctly, that you like the human pup because she rescued you *and* because you think she looks at pictures."

"I like her because she looked at *me*," said Mary, "and she tried to understand what being me is like."

Andrew couldn't help it, he laughed. "*Ha ha ha ha ha!* All right, Mary Mouse, I think I'm beginning to follow you. You're not actually crazy. You're just in the grip of a big idea. I've been there myself, which is why I will help you. But what exactly is the plan?"

Mary thumped her forepaws in frustration. "I don't know! And I can't possibly"—she yawned—"think about it now. I can barely keep my eyes open."

Chapter Thirty-Eight

After Carolyn had gone, Mrs. George closed the top drawer of her desk, leaned back in her chair, and looked out the window. On full display were summer's charms, blue sky, cotton-ball clouds, a red-breasted robin on a telephone wire.

But Mrs. George saw only the content of her soul, and it was cold and black.

Pretty Helen Loviscky was the oldest of six children and the apple of her father's eye. He was fun-loving and hand-some...till the coal dust robbed him of his health. In pain and despair, he drank. One winter night, coming home after a spree, he slid on a patch of ice, fell and hit his head. He never woke up.

Helen was devastated, but family demands left her no time to indulge in grief. She quit school to take care of her siblings and the house while her mother went out to work, cleaning for rich people and bringing home stories about their beautiful possessions and their beautiful lives, kindling envy in the heart of an eldest daughter who wore ragged clothes and cried herself to sleep from exhaustion.

In a way, Carolyn McKay had reminded Mrs. George of herself. Both were bereft after the loss of a parent, both determined to make the world right again through sheer effort of will. In their minds, any mistake was disastrous—caused the cosmos to spin out of control. Even now, this anxious and single-minded determination was Mrs. George's emotional reality. Because of it, she understood Carolyn...and how to manipulate her.

But now obedient, reliable, responsible Carolyn was about to betray her. The child did not realize it herself yet, but it was true. Assaulted by the child's own powers of reason and observation, the myth of the good Mrs. George would melt away, and when it did, Carolyn would communicate her suspicions to others, perhaps even to Frank Kittaning.

Mrs. George didn't like the deed she was contemplating. It was distasteful and, worse yet, a risk. But it was safer than allowing Carolyn to remain at Cherry Street. Mrs. George reminded herself that she hadn't achieved her place in the world by succumbing to sentiment. She had always done what she needed to do to advance and protect her own interests, and she would do so now.

Mrs. George looked away from the window and toward her desk. Then she picked up the telephone and dialed 0.

"Operator?" she said shortly. "I want to place a long-distance call."

Chapter Thirty-Nine

Rather than sleeping in her own nest every day, Mary had been trying out new ones to see how they suited her, With the colony gone, there were plenty to choose from. That day's sleeping quarters once had been occupied by a first-generation daughter of Randolph's. Mary had been attracted by the fluffy bedding. On awakening, she noticed there was something else to appreciate: a picture of a full-grown human female wearing a red scarf around the fur on her head. The female's paw was upraised to show off the muscles of her foreleg; she looked directly at the viewer; her expression was resolute.

There were words on the picture, and after Mary had groomed herself, she went to wake Andrew, then brought him back to read the words aloud.

"It says, 'We can do it,'" Andrew explained, "which is an excellent motto to inspire us. Now, shall we try the dining room for breakfast? I believe they had fresh bread at dinner."

On their way, the two mice stopped off at the main larder and selected dry comestibles to round out their foraging. Mary took a shriveled kernel of corn. Andrew gnawed the head off a petrified ant. Once they had arrived in the dining room wall, Mary said, "It's my turn."

"But I don't mind," said Andrew.

"Nor do I," said Mary, and before he could argue further, she squeezed through the portal. From elsewhere in the home came the sounds of human activity, but by this time of the evening, the dining room was deserted. Knowing where Jimmy sat, Mary checked first beneath his chair and was rewarded with an ample supply of bread crumbs, the best of them coated in margarine.

When she returned, Andrew made a fuss over her skills.

"With only the two of us here, it's so easy a pup could do it," said Mary. "But let us get to work on a plan. How do we communicate what we know to Caro?"

"Can she read?" Andrew asked.

"Of course," said Mary loyally. "She's exceptionally bright."

"Then I have an idea," said Andrew, and it turned out to be so simple, Mary wondered why she had not thought of it herself. Given the human pups' schedule, however, they would have to wait till morning to carry it out.

Meanwhile, it was time for their nightly spy mission on the third floor.

Chapter Forty

The boss's mate had yet to arrive when Andrew and Mary posted themselves beneath the overhang of the kitchen cupboards. The boss herself was seated with a book in her lap, but she was not reading. Rather, she picked the book up, laid it down again, and mumbled, "Of all nights for him to be late."

Finally, Mary felt the quaking of the floorboards that meant the judge was on the stairs. The predator heard it, too, and looked up from his cushion on the sofa. Seconds later came the knock at the door, and the boss rose from her chair to answer it.

"Good evening, Judge," she said.

The boss's mate stepped forward and put his arms around her. The mice had observed that she often resisted affectionate gestures, but on this night she did not.

"Do sit down and I'll pour the sherry," she said. "I have a lot to tell you. I'm afraid we may have a problem."

The boss took two glasses and poured a generous amount from the decanter into each. Meanwhile, the judge went through the rigmarole of lighting his cigar, in the process filling the room with a cloud of smoke. Only with the greatest self-control did Mary keep herself from coughing.

At last the two humans were settled. "What happened?" the judge asked.

"Carolyn suspects there may be something irregular about the adoption this week," the boss replied.

"But how...what...did...?" Blink-blink-blink.

The boss waited for her mate to finish stammering, then said, "I underestimated her," and went on to describe her conversation with Caro that morning in her office.

"She is bright," the judge said when the boss was finished.

"Bright enough to make trouble—especially considering Frank Kittaning's interest in her."

"Do you think she would betray you?" the judge asked.

"The risk is there...for me, and for you. So, reluctantly, I made a telephone call."

It was silent for a long moment. Finally, the judge said, "But aren't you fond of the child?"

There was another silence, then a sigh, and finally the boss said, "I can't afford to be fond of her. I've told you about my father, how he abandoned us?"

"I thought he was killed. An accident."

"It amounted to the same thing," said the boss. "He was a drunk. I didn't know it at the time, but his death was the making of me. I learned how to survive because I had to."

"We were speaking of Carolyn," said the judge.

"We were," said the boss. "She'll learn the same hard lesson that I did. You can't count on anyone." When the judge coughed and cleared his throat, she added, "Present company excepted."

"I wonder if you mean that, Helen," said the judge.

"Of course, I do, dear," said the boss. "We need each other."

The judge took a sip from his glass and puffed on his cigar. "It's an awful thing to do to a child."

"We always knew it might be necessary," the boss said. "That's why we forged the necessary, uh...relationships."

"I suppose you're right. You always are," he said. "Now tell me what happened with the infant."

"The baby nurse was here at dawn. The infant was gone before the children rose. I had a telephone call from Miss Grahame's assistant this afternoon. The boy had arrived, and mother and child were getting acquainted."

"I don't suppose she'll be much of a mother," the judge mused.

The boss shrugged. "Many children have bad mothers. This one at least will have the comforts money can buy."

The judge nodded. "Speaking of money?"

The boss smiled thinly—"I was waiting for you to bring that up"—then rose, walked to her writing desk, opened a drawer, and removed two envelopes, one sealed and one unused. With a letter opener, she slit the top of the sealed envelope, removed from it five green pieces of paper, and placed them in the second envelope. Then she reclosed the first one with paper clips, sealed the second one, and tossed it toward her mate.

"You'll see we made out rather well," she said.

Primly, the judge said, "Thank you," and tucked the

envelope into an inner pocket of his jacket. "When will Mr. Puttley's, uh...representative be here?"

"Day after tomorrow—Saturday," said the boss. "I will tell Carolyn tomorrow."

"Tell her?" The judge looked up.

"That she's to be adopted. She will be surprised, certainly— surprised and overjoyed."

Chapter Forty-One

⬥

After the judge departed, the two mice watched Mrs. George place the paper-clipped envelope in her hiding place in the cold white box. Then she retired to her bedroom, and the mice descended to the ground floor, arriving at last at a pleasantly cramped and sawdust-strewn spot in the wall behind the kitchen.

Agitated, Mary began to pace. "Caro is being sent away! I don't understand where it is she's going, but it is someplace terrible. That I know."

The smell of the previous day's cooking combined with rotten garbage made Andrew's mouth water. He wanted lunch, but could see he'd get none until he and Mary had discussed the latest intelligence. Resigned to the delay, he focused his mind on Caro.

"If we're going to help her," he said, "we must remain calm and analyze the situation. It's money in the envelopes; I know about money from watching transactions at the newsstand. The boss traded the newborn—sold him. And her mate helped her in some way related to the papers in the cold white box. His payment was in that envelope she gave him."

Mary agreed and shook her whiskers. "Stealing a pup from its mother for trade! Such wickedness!"

"It's unnatural," said Andrew, "and it must be deemed unnatural by humans as well. That's why they're afraid of getting caught. So, to keep Caro from telling what she knows about the infant, they're sending her away."

"But Caro is not a threat," Mary said. "She still believes the boss is good. That's the heartbreaking part. We have to warn her that the boss is evil. We have to warn her to resist!"

"All right," said Andrew, trying hard to ignore the empty feeling in his stomach. "But how?"

Mary thought for a moment, then said, "It would seem that the money and papers in the hiding place reveal the truth about the newborn pup. What if Caro were to find them?"

Andrew clapped his paws. "Excellent! You've solved the problem. Now can we eat?"

Mary ignored his outburst. "The question," she went on, "is how to tell her where to look. Perhaps if she were to find a key to the boss's apartment? There is one in the ivory-inlaid box."

"Of course," said Andrew. Mice don't use keys themselves, but like all the colony's art thieves he was thoroughly acquainted with the geography of the the desktop plateau. "And . . . ?" he said encouragingly.

"And—what if Caro were to find that key on her pillow at the same time she found our other, uh . . . gift?" Mary said.

"Would she recognize the key?" Andrew asked.

"I think so," said Mary. "The boss's door is the only interior one with a lock. Its key is made of gray metal, and it's a different shape from those for the exterior."

Andrew was daydreaming. The children had eaten spaghetti for dinner. With luck, there would be bits of salty, powdery Parmesan cheese to forage. Andrew could almost taste it. Even as his hunger raged, he asked another question. "Will she know what to do with it?"

"That's the problem." Mary sighed. "I don't suppose you learned to write when you learned to read? The hero Stuart Little could write."

"The hero had the advantage of humans to teach him," Andrew said.

"In other words, you did not learn to write," said Mary.

"No," Andrew admitted.

"Not that reading's a small accomplishment," Mary added.

"Thank you," Andrew said.

"But in that case," Mary went on, "we will have to devise some other means of directing Caro to the boss's hiding place. Doing this will require thought. What do you say if first we eat our lunch?"

"*Ha ha ha ha ha!*" said Andrew. "Excellent idea!"

Chapter Forty-Two

—◈—

It was a car crash that orphaned Jimmy Levine. He was four years old and riding in the backseat when his dad, lighting a cigarette, drove the family's Ford sedan into a truck that had stopped on the highway to allow a groundhog to cross.

Jimmy's parents went through the windshield. This was in 1943, a time before safety glass, seat belts, or airbags. The Levines' only son wasn't in a child seat; those didn't exist yet, either. But Jimmy was lucky and only hit his head. The blow was enough to knock him out—which turned out to be lucky, too, because he never saw the sad sight of his parents' remains, in fact didn't remember the accident at all, only waking up in the hospital, where the nurses gave him ice cream.

With his parents gone, Jimmy's closest relatives were clear out in California. None had the wherewithal or (in truth) the desire to take in a little kid they'd never met. Jimmy would have to go to an orphanage, but here he got lucky one more time. The child welfare officer took a shine to him and got him placed at Cherry Street, the best orphanage in the region. Even so, the boy's first few months were miserable as, day by day, reality sank in: His parents weren't coming back. This strange building full of people he didn't know was now his home.

Then something shifted in his mind and, young as he was, Jimmy came to a profound realization. He had survived the worst thing that could happen to a kid; he could survive anything.

This realization bred confidence, the kind that didn't care what other people thought. So it was that he could be best friends with someone, Caro, who was not only a girl but a goody-two-shoes besides.

Not that being Caro's friend was easy.

Take their recent discussion about reincarnation. Jimmy had read about it in a Superman comic. He grasped the idea right away and decided he wanted to live his next life as a cat like Gallico. He would gladly put up with some old lady petting him in exchange for square meals, a soft sofa cushion for napping, and—most important—no chores.

The other guys in the intermediate dorm understood at once and agreed cats had it made.

But Caro was disgusted. Caro believed in *doing* things, and worse yet, she frequently wanted Jimmy to help.

On Friday morning as the children filed into breakfast, Jimmy caught sight of Caro and immediately knew that something was up. She had a deep furrow in her brow, which meant she was worried, but not only worried—worried and determined to *do* something.

Jimmy was tired just thinking about it. Whatever today's plan was, it was going to be a doozy.

"Talk after breakfast," she whispered to him as they made their way to the line for clean-hands inspection. "It's important."

Mrs. George did not make any announcements that morning, so the children had free time before chores. Caro made a beeline for Jimmy even before he'd left the table.

"Okay, okay—gee whiz. What is it I gotta do now?" Jimmy asked her.

The other boys laughed and elbowed each other.

"Come with me," Caro said, and all but dragged him to the front piano parlor, where they would not be disturbed.

The children did not like the front piano parlor. It was close to the sidewalk, with a picture window. Sometimes passersby peered in or pointed "like we was zoo animals or something," according to Melissa. The furnishings, too, were all wrong—fussy and old-fashioned, uncomfortable for fidgety children.

Jimmy was curious to learn what Caro wanted. But it was beneath his dignity to let her know that. So he dropped down on the settee and made his voice bored and annoyed. "What is it now?"

Caro pulled two things from her pocket. One was a piece of newspaper, which he could look at later. But the other, an old gray metal key, caused his heart to miss a beat. Had Caro lost her mind? She would get them both whipped!

"Where did you get that?" he asked.

"Shhh—keep your voice down," Caro said. "Do you know what it is?"

"I've seen it before," he said. "It belongs in a box on Mrs. George's desk. I think it's a spare for her apartment."

"So that's what they want," Caro said.

"That's what who want? What are you talking about?"

"You won't believe where I got it, or this"—she indicated the paper—"either. I found them on my pillow this morning after I was through washing up."

"One of the girls must've put them there," Jimmy said. "Is somebody mad at you? Are they trying to get you in trouble?"

"That's not it," said Caro, "and please don't say I'm crazy. I think the mouse . . . the one I rescued? I think the mouse put them there. It wants us, that is, me, to do something. But I can't do it alone. You have to help."

Jimmy's jaw dropped in surprise, but a moment later he was laughing so hard that Caro had to kick his shin.

"The mice are talking to you now?" he said when he'd caught his breath. "Oh, Caro. That's a good joke."

"No, listen," said Caro. "You know the fable about the lion and the mouse?"

Jimmy shrugged. "I remember Miss Ragone read to us from that Aesop book."

"The lion spared the mouse's life," Caro reminded him, "and the mouse swore he'd help the lion sometime. The lion thought how could an animal so puny help him—the king of the forest? But then he got caught in a hunter's net, and the mouse gnawed the ropes and set him free."

Jimmy shook his head. The world according to Caro was a lot more complicated than the world according to him.

"Oka-a-ay," he said. "So you're saying the mouse is trying to set you free?"

"I'm saying I helped the mouse, and now it wants to help me. Only I don't know how it wants to help me. But here's the other thing, the more important thing."

She displayed the scrap of paper and told Jimmy how the day before, Mrs. George had shown her the newspaper on her desk, the one with a hole in it. "She said the mice tore it, and I think this must be the piece they took. Look how uneven the edges are. It's because they had to tear it with their teeth, gnaw it."

Jimmy examined the paper and got a queer feeling in his belly. Was it possible Caro wasn't crazy after all? "But why—" he started to ask.

"Read it," she said. "All of it."

Baby Boy Taken

PHILADELPHIA—*Police say a male infant less than 36 hours old may have been taken from the West Lying-In Hospital sometime Wednesday.*

The infant, born to an unmarried woman whose name was not disclosed, disappeared during morning visiting hours. Nursing staff told police the woman's account of the child's disappearance was incoherent as a result of her extreme emotional distress.

Police planned to interview her further today. There were apparently no other witnesses to the baby's disappearance.

The missing infant is a Caucasian male with light hair. Police are asking anyone with knowledge of the baby's whereabouts to please telephone.

Jimmy was not always a fast thinker, but he could put two and two together. "You think this might have something to do with Charlie. But there's lots of babies born in a city every day, aren't there?"

"Probably," Caro said. "But it's a pretty big coincidence that this light-haired baby boy disappeared from a hospital right before Charlie showed up here. And there's something else, too." She explained about the forceps marks and Mrs. George's inconsistent story.

Jimmy thought for a minute. "Let's say you're right. Then who brought him here? Charlie didn't just up and crawl away from the hospital."

"The police brought him," said Caro.

"The police wouldn't bring him here and then tell the newspaper he was missing," Jimmy said. "Something's fishy."

"That's why I wanted to talk it over with you," said Caro. "I'm trying to understand."

Jimmy was flattered that Caro thought he could help her with a puzzle as hard as this one. But could he? He only knew one thing. "Don't say anything else about it to Mrs. George. She might be in on it."

"Oh, Jimmy, no. That's impossible," Caro said. "She's... she's Mrs. George."

"I know everyone thinks she's a saint, but not me," said Jimmy.

"She lost her temper that time, that's all. What I think is that Mrs. George might be in trouble, and the mice want us to help her."

"That's nonsense, Caro. Why do the mice want to help *her*? She hates them! She called the exterminator!" Jimmy said.

Caro put her hands on her head and squeezed her eyes closed. "I know it doesn't make sense. Nothing makes sense— except one thing. We have to do one thing."

Uh-oh. Here it came. "What's that?" Jimmy asked.

"Use this key," said Caro.

Jimmy's heart went *thud*. Was she serious? If they were caught, the boss wouldn't just whip them, she would *behead* them. But before he could argue, Matron Polly appeared in the doorway.

"Oh, there you are, Caro. As for you, Jimmy, aren't you late again?"

"I'm going now," said Jimmy.

Caro said, "I'm sorry. I know my chore today is laundry."

"Not right now it isn't," said Matron. "Mrs. George wants to see you . . . again." Then she smiled. "I think it's good news."

Chapter Forty-Three

In the few hours since Caro had awakened that day, she had learned that baby Charlie had been kidnapped and—more amazing still—that mice were leaving her communications.

For one brain in one morning, that should have been enough. But now there was something new.

She was going to be adopted!

By the time she left Mrs. George's office a few minutes later, the poor child felt entirely overwhelmed.

A man—a nice man, according to Mrs. George—would arrive by automobile the very next morning to drive her.

"A family of your own, Carolyn. Think of that!" Mrs. George had said.

And she had gone on to paint a beautiful picture. A mama and a papa. Two little sisters. A big house with trees and fields all around.

It was wonderful!

It was scary.

Caro's whole life, everything she had known for five long years, was about to change. And change was hard.

Stunned as she was, Caro had still asked questions, and Mrs. George had done her best to answer. They were a loving family. They wanted a responsible older girl, someone to help look after the little ones.

"They want me for a servant?" Caro had said.

"No, no, dear. They want a daughter, an eldest daughter, a helpful daughter—someone just like you. I believe perhaps their own dear daughter...died."

"How sad," Caro had said.

"But not sad for you," Mrs. George had said. "Fortunate."

"But I don't understand," Caro had said. "How did they know about me? I've never even met them! Do they live here in Philadelphia?"

"They live in another state," said Mrs. George vaguely. "There are other homes like ours elsewhere in the country, and sometimes we directors are in touch with one another. When I learned that there was a God-fearing, well-off family seeking a responsible girl to adopt, I thought of you. I've had to keep it quiet until now, until the details were worked out. But all that's completed. I'm giving you a wonderful opportunity."

Caro was so astonished, she hardly followed Mrs. George's explanation of practical matters—how she was to travel, what belongings she could take—until one fact penetrated her confusion: She was to leave tomorrow! A man, a friend of the family, would pick her up early. She should say her good-byes to the children and to the staff that very night.

"You are excused from chores for the rest of the day," Mrs. George had said. "I'm sure you have things to do, things to pack up. Matron will help you."

"Oh, no, ma'am. Thank you very much, but I don't want to be excused from chores," Caro had said. "The other girls will have more to do then, and laundry is hard work, and that wouldn't be fair. And anyway—"

"Yes?"

Caro shrugged. "It won't take me long to pack my things, ma'am. I don't have very much."

Of all the chores at Cherry Street, laundry was the most despised. The washing machine, wringer, ironing board, washbasins, and clotheslines were all in the basement, which was clean and tidy but miserably hot and humid in the summer. The work itself was hard, too. Wet linens were heavy. Scouring stains made your shoulders ache and left your hands raw. The girls joked that the clothes were washed not only in water but in their own sweat.

Ironing was the worst job of the worst. Automatic irons had been invented in the 1920s, but in 1949 they were not yet reliable or universally used. Steam irons were a thing of the distant future.

The girls at Cherry Street had an old-fashioned iron, one that was heated on a stove and used until it cooled off, at which point it was heated on the stove again. Pushing an iron across cotton fabric was hot, muscular, and exacting labor. A moment's inattention and you burned yourself or—and this was almost worse—scorched the fabric.

With her disfigured right hand, Caro could have begged off ironing altogether, but she never would, and that day a pile of boys' button-down cotton shirts awaited her.

"You were late yesterday and you're late again today. You're gonna get in trouble," Melissa said. She was nearest to Caro, rotating the handle of the wringer, whose rollers squeezed the water out of bedsheets so that they would dry faster.

Caro didn't answer because she wasn't listening, so Melissa repeated herself.

"What? Yes, yes, I suppose I'm going to get in trouble," Caro said at last. Mrs. George hadn't told her to keep the news a secret, but she wanted Jimmy to be the first to know. Before she could sort out her thoughts, she had to talk to him.

The morning passed slowly—one shirt following another, the other girls' conversations swirling around and annoying her with their triviality. At one point, Caro was tempted to shout: "I'm leaving! I've been adopted! What do you think of that?"

And what would they think of it?

Would they envy her?

Yes, of course. Just as she would envy any child who was getting a family of her own.

But they would also miss her. And she would miss them, too.

Thinking of it, she felt tears well in her eyes. They were her family now, or the closest thing she had to one. Would they write to her? Would they forget her? She would never forget them.

But still, she didn't say anything, and Barbara teased her for being lost in her own thoughts. Caro didn't respond, which caused the other intermediate girls to look at one another and shrug. It was no fun teasing if you didn't get a reaction.

Finally, it was lunchtime. The girls had ten minutes to wash before they filed into the dining room. Afterward, Caro could not have told what it was she ate; she had put the fork in her mouth mechanically, the same way she'd ironed the shirts, all the time waiting for the moment when she could talk to Jimmy.

The two friends met again in the front piano parlor and, all in a rush, she told him...and before she had even finished, he was shaking his head. "It's a trick—don't you see? It's just like Charlie. He disappeared and now you will, too!"

"What?" Caro felt dazed. "No, Mrs. George wouldn't—"

"Mrs. George wouldn't, Mrs. George wouldn't...nyah nyah nyah, Caro. You're wrong and she would. She's crooked and a liar and you don't see it!"

Caro had never seen Jimmy like this—near tears, he was so frustrated. Instinctively, she tried to comfort him, but that only made things worse. "Of course you don't want me to go. I don't want to leave you, either. Don't you think I'm scared, too?"

"Does the family know about your scars?" Jimmy asked cruelly.

Caro didn't answer right away. "I don't know. I didn't think to ask."

It was Jimmy's turn to take a breath. "I'm sorry, Caro. I didn't mean that. I'm just trying to make you listen to me. You can't trust her. You can't. What's happened with Charlie proves it."

Caro didn't know what to say. Jimmy was wrong; she was sure of that. He was reacting this way because he was envious. Any of the orphans would be.

Chapter Forty-Four

Threatened by a feline, a rodent always flees in terror. This was the natural order; every creature knew it. So when the other night in the kitchen that mouse female had turned on Gallico and bared her teeth, it was entirely reasonable that he had been startled.

Not scared.

Never scared.

Merely startled.

That rodent had been lucky to escape with her life. The one in the boss's living room now would not be. It wasn't only anticipation of a bloody, tasty snack that excited Gallico. It was also his desire to exact revenge.

Moments before, the cat had been at his usual post on the boss's sofa when the sound of breaking glass awakened him. He rolled over. He looked up. What he saw astonished him. On the wood floor beneath the boss's writing desk was a small broken bottle, its liquid contents spilled to form a brilliant blue puddle in which a mouse seemed to be wading.

Stupid, clumsy rodent, Gallico thought. Having knocked the bottle from the desk to the floor and broken it, she didn't know enough to stay out of the mess. When the boss returned and saw the stain, the boss would be apoplectic. If Gallico did not want to be blamed, he had better be well out of the way by then.

But first, he had a murder to attend to.

Eyes never leaving his prey, the big cat positioned himself and waited patiently for her to come out into the open where he would have a clear shot. Meanwhile, the rodent—her paws sticky, wet and blue—marched boldly and deliberately across the rug toward the kitchen.

Gallico gathered his legs beneath him, swished his tail once, twice, and . . . wait a second.

From across the kitchen floor came a second rodent, this one a large male and at least as stupid as the first, squeaking for all the world as if he wanted to pose a challenge: "Look! Look at me! I'm over here!"

Trying to decide which mouse to dispose of first, Gallico mistimed his jump and overshot. Rather than landing his claws on the rodent's neck, he landed his belly there.

No matter, thought Gallico. *Decapitated or smothered, you're dead either way.*

The mouse, however, had other ideas. She did not succumb but bit the cat—actually bit him on the belly!—causing Gallico to howl in pain and protest before rolling his big body away. All the time the second mouse, the male, continued his diversionary tactics.

Cartwheels! Somersaults! Flips!

If he was trying to get the cat's attention, he was succeeding—as well as hastening his own demise. As the female continued her stately procession toward the big white box where the boss kept food, Gallico aimed at the male and prepared to strike...but another distraction presented itself, the sound of human footfalls on the stairs.

It was not the boss. It was Matron Polly, paying her afternoon visit.

Mrrreeeow! Gallico's frustration was complete. He must abandon his prey or be blamed for the blue spillage, which by now had expanded beyond the desk. In fact, those infernal rodents had left blue tracks everywhere.

Moments later, safely hidden beneath the boss's bed, Gallico heard Matron Polly turn her key in the lock, heard her enter the apartment, heard her squeal.

She had seen the rodent!

Perhaps she would succeed where he had failed?

But she was much too slow. Gallico heard her moving about and muttering, "Oh—what a mess with all this ink! Well, one thing's for certain. Yours truly is not cleaning it up. Far as I know, things were spic, span, and tidy when last I was here."

Polly's visits to the boss's apartment were predictable. Today, as usual, she went into the kitchen and opened the white box. But instead of closing it immediately, she uttered an inarticulate cry and then, "Ha! Serves you right, you little beast!" After that the door slammed, and she said, "That'll be a cold coffin for you."

The remaining noises were familiar—chair creaking, bottle opening, the susurration of the bottle's contents. Then it was quiet but for Polly's single comment: "What a surprise that will be for Her Majesty—a tiny mouse in her Frigidaire, cold, stiff, and dead."

Chapter Forty-Five

The adults at the Cherry Street Children's Home had their share of secrets, most of them well known to the children.

For example, the children all knew—even Annabelle—that Matron Polly took a half-hour break each afternoon to drink a bottle of beer in Mrs. George's private apartment. They had seen her going up the stairs. They had seen her coming back. They had smelled the beer on her breath and seen the bottles lined up for return to the store. They knew she was more cheerful after her break than before, so after was a better time to ask for a favor.

The children also knew about the judge's visits. Among the older ones, these visits were a source of both fascination and disgust. Ned claimed to have stolen the spare key from the boss's desk, unlocked her apartment, sneaked inside, and tried a sip of the light brown liquid they drank—sherry, it was called. He said it tasted vile.

Finally, the children knew that Mrs. George left the home each day between three and six in the afternoon to run errands and pay calls. This last was not a secret, but it did mean that the grown-up population was reliably diminished by one during those hours—a fact that could sometimes be used to advantage.

Such was Jimmy's plan that afternoon. But if he and Caro were going to unlock the boss's apartment with the key the mice had left, he would need cooperation from the olders and the intermediates. To win them over, he had made a post-lunchtime circuit of the dormitories, the parlors, and the yard outside.

"Listen." He had made his voice conspiratorial. "I got something I gotta do I can't talk about yet, but I'll fill you in later. It's in the boss's apartment. And the thing is, obviously, I need to be sure I'm not bothered."

"You want us to warn you if the boss comes back early?" Ricky had asked.

"The boss or anybody that might happen to go upstairs. We're going in after Matron's done with her beer."

"We?" Ricky had repeated.

"Me and Caro," Jimmy said. Then, to forestall teasing, he added, "It's something secret. Caro found out about it."

"What's the secret?" Ricky had asked.

"A *secret*," Jimmy had said. He could only imagine the reaction if he told them he was following instructions from a mouse. "You'll help, right? Three bangs for the boss. One for anybody else."

When Mr. and Mrs. C. Philips-Bodbetter installed the hot-water heating system, they had not considered its usefulness for emergency communications. The children, however, had figured this out immediately. Anytime anything metallic struck a radiator, it could be heard throughout the home—even in the boss's apartment.

Jimmy was good at talking, and by the time he was done, everyone had agreed to be on the lookout.

Shortly before four o'clock, just after Matron Polly had returned downstairs, Caro and Jimmy stood on the third-floor landing. With the old-fashioned key in her hand, Caro looked at Jimmy for courage. He nodded. She put the key into the lock, turned it, and pushed the door, which opened without a sound.

Neither Caro nor Jimmy had ever been inside Mrs. George's apartment. Of the orphans, only Ned had. The apartment was not large, and the door opened directly into the parlor, which was neat and cozy. Two doorways, one to the kitchen and one to the bedroom, led out of it. A writing desk stood to the left of the entry door. The sight of Gallico, napping on the chintz sofa, made the scene peaceful.

"How do we know what to do now?" Caro whispered.

"You don't have to whisper," Jimmy said out loud. "There's nobody around."

"I'd rather whisper," said Caro.

It was Jimmy who spotted the broken inkwell. It had fallen onto the wood floor, splashing its contents there and on the rug, too. "Is that a clue?" Jimmy asked.

Caro grimaced. "It's a sticky mess, but look." She pointed to a line of ink spots that traced a path toward the kitchen doorway.

Jimmy knelt to get a closer look and grinned. "Little paw prints," he said, "left by your friend the mouse, I guess." He shook his head. "After today, nothing will ever surprise me again. Come on."

Feeling like the intruder she was, Caro tiptoed across the room. Jimmy, in contrast, strolled with arms and legs swinging, claiming the territory for himself.

The paw prints became fainter the farther they moved from the overturned ink bottle. Then, in the middle of the kitchen floor, they became smeared and chaotic—as if the mouse had turned around and something…

Jimmy and Caro had the same thought at the same time and looked up at Gallico. Was he really sleeping so innocently? Or had he been watching them?

"Let's take a look," said Jimmy.

The children turned toward the sofa. Gallico looked up and scrambled to get away—but too slowly to evade Jimmy's hands. *Mrrree-ow!*

"Guilty conscience," said Jimmy.

"Don't hurt him," said Caro.

"He wouldn't've thought twice about hurting your mouse," Jimmy said; then, with a deft motion, he flipped the cat over, revealing ink splotches on his belly.

Caro let loose with a squeal, then hastily covered her mouth and whispered, "Oh, you wicked cat, how could you?"

Jimmy shook his head. "I don't think he did. There isn't any blood, and the mouse tracks keep going. I think he tried, but the mouse escaped."

Jimmy dropped Gallico onto the sofa, where he began furiously to wash his face.

Back in the kitchen, the children saw that the paw-print trail culminated at the base of the electric refrigerator.

Again, they looked at each other. Then Jimmy nodded, and Caro pulled the silver latch.

Chapter Forty-Six

———⟫◦⟪———

Mary had never been so cold. To stay warm, she exercised—running in circles in the darkness, tripping and stumbling over comestibles that at any other time she would have been delighted to sample.

What kept her from losing heart was thinking of Stuart Little. He had also been trapped in an electric refrigerator, he had also exercised to keep warm, and he had emerged with only a case of bronchitis...whatever that was.

Even knowing the story of Stuart, Mary was startled by the noise, the rush of air, and the brilliant light when at last the door was opened. For a moment, she was blind, and then she saw to her joy and relief that it was the human pups looking in at her. The plan had worked! They had followed the trail of ink!

Caro spoke first. "Oh, dear, you must be nearly frozen!"

"Well, I am, as a matter of fact," said Mary.

"Poor little critter," said Jimmy. "I think it's hysterical."

"Who are you calling 'critter'?" asked Mary.

"It wants to tell us something," said Caro.

"You're right about that," said Mary.

The boss's hiding place was in a separate space behind a door at the top of the refrigerator box. If the children didn't

open the door and look inside, all Mary and Andrew's efforts had been in vain. Anxious to convey this last bit of intelligence, Mary stretched to the utmost on her hind legs and extended her forepaws to point out the door.

"Its paws are blue!" said Jimmy.

"That's just the ink," said Caro. "I think it wants us to look in the freezer."

"Freezer—that's it!" Mary squeaked, and now—work done—she sneezed and began to shiver in earnest. She would not wait to see the human pups' reaction when they looked inside. She had to warm up soon or risk falling sick. So she dropped lightly from one shelf to the next until she reached the floor.

"Wait!" Caro looked down. "Why did you leave us the key? Where is Charlie—do you know? Is Mrs. George in trouble? Is it . . . is it like the Aesop's fable?"

Cold as she was, Mary turned back and studied the pup that loomed above her. *I wonder if she is considered attractive,* Mary thought. To mice, all humans—with their gross size, strange allocation of fur, inadequate ears, and complete lack of tail and whiskers—looked similar and similarly ugly. And their smell, which was comforting at a distance, was rank when you got close.

For an instant, Mary questioned her decision to help humans at all, but then her eyes met Caro's and she saw kindness, intelligence, and . . . yes, wonder.

"I would answer if only you could understand," she said. "And I would ask you questions of my own. Who is Louisa May Alcott? And why do humans kill mice but feed predators?"

Caro looked at Jimmy. "The mouse is talking to us, Jimmy. I know it it is. If only we could understand."

"If only you could," said Mary. "Now look in the hiding place; don't trust the boss, and scurry safe—both of you!"

Then she spun around, flipped her tail, and disappeared into the gap between the cupboard doors.

Chapter Forty-Seven

"She's leaving!" With her pinkie finger, Caro waved good-bye, but she was too late; already the soft gray form was gone. "Where is it going, do you think?"

"Search me," Jimmy said. "Maybe there's a whole kingdom of 'em in the walls."

"Do you really think so?" For a moment, Caro was so charmed by the thought, she forgot where she and Jimmy were standing and why.

Jimmy shrugged. "After all that's happened today, why not? But look, we've got to hurry, Caro. Ready?"

Caro nodded. Jimmy reached for the handle and pulled open the freezer door. Refrigerator freezers were becoming widespread in 1949, and corporations were stepping up to provide people with foods to fill them. Besides two aluminum trays filled with ice, Mrs. George's contained three boxes of Birds Eye frozen peas, two cans of Minute Maid frozen orange juice concentrate, and a stack of square packets full of something—meat, probably—wrapped neatly in white butcher paper.

Caro shook her head, disappointed. Jimmy said, "I don't get it."

"Unless…?" Feeling bold, Caro reached in and removed

one of the white packets. In her hand, the contents did not feel like meat but like sheets of paper. Caro couldn't risk looking inside. She knew she'd never rewrap the packet the same way, which would tell Mrs. George that someone had been there.

Wondering what more she could do, Caro noticed something else—an envelope on top of the second packet. Jimmy saw it, too, and didn't hesitate. He took it, detached the three paper clips, pulled it open, and looked.

What Caro saw inside the envelope almost stopped her heart in her chest—hundred-dollar bills! Caro had never in her life seen even one, and here was a whole stack!

Jimmy fumbled the envelope—in the process dropping a paper clip to the floor—and stared. "If this was ours, we could have anything...go anywhere...Caro, let's take it! Let's take it and run. *Please?* We wouldn't be orphans anymore. No one would know."

Jimmy's blue eyes were wide, and for an instant, Caro's mind went blank. Then it flashed thoughts at her in frenzied succession: *Jimmy doesn't care about my scars. He likes me just because I'm Caro. He wants me to go with him.*

It's too scary. It's too dangerous.

But all that money? We would be all right. We would be far away. We would be like a family, a family of two.

Finally, she blinked and said, "We can't. It isn't ours."

"It isn't hers, either, I bet—the old witch," Jimmy said. "She stole it or something. Otherwise, why is she hiding it?"

Caro shook her head. No. She wouldn't believe it. In an

uncertain world, you had to believe in something, and Caro believed in Mrs. George. There was a good explanation for the money. There had to be.

Clank! Clank! Clank! The sound of the alarm made them both jump.

"The boss—she's coming!" Hurriedly, Jimmy clipped the envelope and slammed the freezer shut.

"Wait—you missed one." Caro retrieved the third paper clip from the floor, opened the freezer, and—fumbling a little—affixed it. Then she laid the white paper packet on top so that the freezer would look just as they had found it.

After that, the two children ran. In the doorway, Caro turned back and took one step inside. Gallico was asleep on the sofa once again. Mrs. George would be furious about the spilled ink, but she wouldn't associate it with the children. Was there any possible clue to their visit?

Nothing she could see.

Outside on the landing, Jimmy locked the door, and then, for a few seconds, the two stood and listened. All was quiet, so, on tiptoes, Caro and Jimmy hurried down the stairs.

Chapter Forty-Eight

———◆———

Mrs. George had completed her Friday calls with unusual efficiency and thought she might indulge herself with a brief nap before dinner. The last few days had been difficult. With so much on her mind, she had not slept well.

Before going upstairs, Mrs. George paid a visit to the kitchen. There she reminded Mrs. Spinelli that the exterminators were coming after breakfast in the morning and the children would be spending the day at Fairmount Park. They would need packed lunches.

Mrs. Spinelli responded with her usual truculence. Ascending the stairs, Mrs. George thought certainly there must be a reliable cook somewhere with a more accommodating disposition. If such a person could be found, she would be quite happy to give Mrs. Spinelli her walking papers.

Upstairs in her apartment at last, Mrs. George advanced only a few steps before she spotted blue blotches on the carpet—ink, it looked like. What in the name of...?

She turned back toward the door, surveyed her writing desk, the broken inkwell, the mess on the floor...and forgot all about taking a nap. She was wide awake now—and angry.

The cat! He knew he was in trouble, too. He was hiding. And Mrs. George knew where.

"Gotcha!" She reached under her bed, gripped the scruff of Gallico's neck, pulled him roughly into the light, and held him up.

He was too scared to protest. As expected, she found ink...but it was on his abdomen instead of his paws.

Why would that be?

Mrs. George dropped the cat to the carpet and aimed a kick, but Gallico was prepared and scooted back under the bed, out of her way.

"I'll deal with you later," she said, and then returned to the parlor, where she knelt to examine the line of spots on the carpet and the wood floor. They looked like smudges, but they might have been animal tracks. Whatever they were, she now saw, they were too small to have been made by a cat.

Could it be those detestable mice?

The more she thought, the more likely that seemed. A mouse must have knocked over the ink bottle by chance, then made the tracks on its way to the kitchen in search of food.

Mrs. George was still angry. But there was some comfort in knowing the mice would get their just deserts in the morning. As for the cat, maybe he wasn't to blame for the ink, but she did not regret her outburst. Any decent cat would have done his job and caught the mice. Once again, Gallico had let her down.

Mrs. George's cleaning supplies were kept in the pantry closet beyond the kitchen. She retrieved what she needed—a bucket, detergent, a rag, rubber gloves—then went back to the parlor and began to scrub.

It was only when she was down on her hands and knees addressing the stain by the writing desk that she noticed something...another footprint outlined in blue ink. It had not been made by a cat or a mouse but by a shoe, and the shoe was not her own. It was a child's shoe, and it belonged to someone who had stolen into her apartment while she was out.

Chapter Forty-Nine

Jimmy couldn't believe his ears. Even now that she'd seen the money, Caro wouldn't listen to reason.

"Mrs. George is doing some kind of organized crime deals—like Bugsy Siegel," he argued. "There's a lot of gangsters in Philadelphia, Caro. You can read about 'em in the paper any day. Who else hides that kind of money in the kitchen instead of putting it in the bank?"

"Mrs. George is no gangster," Caro said. "You only have to look at her to see that. You are talking nonsense."

"Oh, I am?" Jimmy said. "Well, you talk to mice, so I'd say we're even. Either way, you're not leaving tomorrow. We have to get to the bottom of this first."

The two children were in the front piano parlor, where they had gone for privacy after coming downstairs. The furniture in that room had belonged to Mrs. Philips-Bodbetter's mother. When she died, Mrs. Philips-Bodbetter had ordered it sent to Cherry Street because it did not match the decorating scheme of her modern house. Now Caro threw herself so vigorously onto an antique settee that its walnut joints creaked. Then she looked up at Jimmy, and there were tears in her eyes.

"I have to believe, don't you understand? This is the only chance for a real family I will ever have."

Jimmy was scared seeing Caro like this and decided to lay off. But that didn't mean he was giving up. Whatever Mrs. George had planned for the next day, it was a trap. He wouldn't let Mrs. George spring it on his friend. He would find some way to stop her.

"I have to pack," Caro said after a moment. "But there's one other thing. The exterminator."

Jimmy saw what she meant. The mice had helped them or tried to anyway. It was their turn to help the mice. "But what do we do?" he asked.

"I have an idea," Caro said. "You'll have to work fast... while Mrs. George is still upstairs."

She explained, and he agreed. Then he made her promise to meet him later.

"But when?" Caro asked. "There's supposed to be a going-away gathering after dinner. That's what Matron Polly told me."

"After that, then," Jimmy insisted.

"Okay," Caro said. "Right before lights-out. We can meet back here."

Caro's instructions required Jimmy to go first to Mrs. George's office and after that to find Melissa. She was in the north parlor reading the new Archie comic book—this one with Jughead on the cover. Jimmy was grateful she was by herself.

"Use the telephone?" Melissa's eyes widened when he told her what he wanted. "But . . . I've never dialed one before, let alone spoken into it. I wouldn't know how."

"It's easy. I'll dial for you. Then I'll give you the receiver, and you talk into it like you're talking to me."

"But how do you even know what telephone number to dial?" Melissa asked. Jimmy showed her the paper where he'd written it down. She was impressed, but she was not done arguing. "I don't like mice any more than anybody else does," she said.

"We're not doing it for the mice, exactly," Jimmy said. "We're doing it for Caro. And before you ask, I can't tell you why. Maybe later I can."

Melissa teased him. "Jimmy: Man of Mystery—it sounds like a new radio hero." She shrugged, rolled her comic book into a tube, and stood up. "Okay, sure, why not? What's a few more demerits?"

It wasn't really in Jimmy's vocabulary to say thank you. So he didn't. He just started walking. "Mrs. Spinelli has a telephone in her office. She won't hear us. She's too busy clanking pots while she makes dinner. Come on."

The cook's office was in the back corner of the home, across a narrow service hallway from the kitchen. For the second time that afternoon, Jimmy was entering unfamiliar territory. In summer, it was stifling hot in this part of the ground floor when Mrs. Spinelli was cooking, and Jimmy felt his shirt dampen with sweat.

The door to the closet-sized office was open, probably for ventilation. Inside, the desk was tidy, the only paper on the blotter a neatly written list for the coming week's grocery delivery. The black telephone was beside the blotter.

Jimmy had gotten the number from the address book Mrs. George kept on her desk: Delaware 2-2618. Now he looked at the dial on the telephone. The truth was, he had never used a telephone, either, but it seemed as if it should be easy. He knew he was supposed to dial 3 and 3, which corresponded with *D* and *E* for *Delaware*—then the rest of the number. He put his finger in the hole next to the 3 and brought the dial around till it stopped.

"I think you have to lift up the receiver first," Melissa whispered. "Then you listen for a hum. That's the dial tone."

"Sure," Jimmy said. "I knew that."

He tried again. The process—twisting the dial, releasing it, and waiting as it fell back—seemed to take forever, but at last the seven digits were complete. Then—as if it were a hot potato—he handed the receiver to Melissa, who put it to her ear and frowned.

This part also seemed to take forever. Why wasn't Melissa talking? Wasn't there anybody at the other end to answer the telephone? He had a terrible thought. Could the business be closed? If it was closed—what would happen then?

Finally—to Jimmy's great relief—Melissa spoke, and her voice was an uncanny imitation of the boss's. "Hello? Yes, hello? This is Mrs. Helen George at the Cherry Street Children's Home. I wish to cancel the services of your exterminator gentleman who previously was appointed to come here tomorrow morning." There was a pause, and she said, "Yes, that is correct. And you are mighty welcome, for sure. Good-bye."

Melissa hung up the receiver, took a deep breath, let it out, and grinned. "I did it!"

"Why did it take so long before anybody answered?" Jimmy asked.

"She said she was the after-hours answering service," said Melissa. "She said she'd make sure they got the message."

Jimmy sighed with relief. He had put on a good show for Melissa, but really he had been scared of failing and scared of getting caught. They could still get caught if they didn't hurry.

For the length of time it took Jimmy and Melissa to return to the foyer from Mrs. Spinelli's office, they reveled in their accomplishment. Once in the foyer, however, they realized that something had happened, something strange. Except for the girls on kitchen duty, all the children were gathered there, along with Matron Polly and Mr. Donald. It was unnaturally quiet, and everyone looked worried.

"What is it?" Melissa asked Betty.

Betty shook her head. "We don't understand it, either, but the boss asked Matron to look at all the girls' shoes."

"Our shoes?" Melissa couldn't help looking down at her own, which were lace-up oxfords, same as everyone else's— nothing remarkable about them. "Do I have to show her mine?"

Betty shook her head. "Not anymore. She must've found what she was looking for. Matron sent Caro to the boss's office. She hasn't come out yet."

"But what's the matter?" Melissa asked. "I don't understand."

Betty bit her lip. "It's something bad, Melissa. The boss was in a fury. I've never seen her like that."

Chapter Fifty

———◆———

Caro was not at dinner.

And Mrs. George did not come in to make announcements.

Instead, it was Matron Polly who told the children about their field trip to the park the next day. They would leave early because the exterminator was coming to take care of the mouse problem.

Melissa and Jimmy looked at each other, but neither smiled. After what had happened since their telephone call, they didn't feel like smiling.

"Where's Caro?" It was Ricky who asked Matron Polly the question they were all thinking. Dinner was over, but the children were still seated at the two long tables in the dining room. Standing before them, Matron Polly looked uncomfortable.

"I believe she is with Mrs. George," Matron Polly said.

"But why?" Barbara asked.

"And why did she pack her things?" asked Virginia.

"And what's the matter with her shoes?" asked Annabelle.

Matron Polly, usually the most placid of women, lost her temper. "Carolyn has been adopted. She is leaving tomorrow morning. I believe she is spending her last evening with Mrs. George in her private apartment. That's all I know. Now, you children—you be quiet, all of you. It's nothing to do with you. *You hear me?*"

Adopted!

Imagine that! Sure, she was nice as could be, but she had those awful scars!

And why was it a secret? Weren't they going to say good-bye? It almost never happened that older children were adopted, but when it did, they always said good-bye.

Disconsolate and puzzled, the children dispersed. It was still light outside, and some of the boys went out to the yard to play kickball. Jimmy would have been among them, but instead he went back to the intermediate boys' dorm, lay down on his bed, and stared at the ceiling.

Alone among the children, he knew exactly what had happened. Caro must have stepped in the ink. Mrs. George had seen the footprint, looked for the ink-stained shoe, found it. So Mrs. George knew that Caro had been in her apartment today, but Caro had not told her that Jimmy had been there, too. If Caro had told her, by now Jimmy would be in trouble, too.

Caro was loyal, a true friend.

But now where was she? Hidden somewhere, most likely. Mrs. George must be afraid she might say something to someone else about what she had found. Tomorrow, Caro would be safely out of the way. She would disappear...just like Charlie.

Jimmy didn't believe in any nice family with two little girls. He knew more about these things than Caro. He knew from the other boys that there were orphanages much different from Cherry Street, ones that took kids in and made them work like slaves, didn't even send them to school.

Was Mrs. George such a monster that she would send Caro to a place like that?

Jimmy was independent, self-sufficient, and accustomed to making his own way. But right now, he felt hopeless and alone. Wherever Caro was tonight, Mrs. George was not going to let Jimmy near her. And tomorrow would be too late. A man was coming in an automobile to take Caro away.

With Melissa's help, Jimmy had saved the mice. But how was he going to save Caro?

Wait a minute. *With Melissa's help*... Jimmy had the beginning of an idea. Maybe there was something he could do.

Chapter Fifty-One

Bayard Boudreau thought of himself as a driver, and when some acquaintance at the bar chanced to ask how he made his living, that was what he answered. There was a little more to it, but no sense alarming his new friend or taking the chance he might be a cop or, worse, FBI.

Bayard had also noticed, over the years, that a certain type of accommodating lady was impressed by the pistol in his jacket. Whether the lady took him to be lawman or outlaw didn't necessarily matter, and he didn't go to great lengths to clarify, either.

Bayard had never stopped to think much about what some might call the moral implications of the business enterprise of which he was a part. It was illegal, he knew that, and because he regularly had to cross state lines, he could be put away for a lot of years if he was dumb enough to let the feds catch him. But he figured the right or wrong of running a workhouse for kids nobody wanted was not up to him. That was Mr. Puttley's lookout.

Anyway, he had only had to use his gun in the line of work the one time when the kid tried to pull a penknife on him. The look of fear on the brat's face when he saw the gun had been downright comical. And he hadn't actually shot the kid. Mr. Puttley wouldn't have liked that. A swift blow to the temple with the gun butt had been enough. After that, the brat was quiet as could be.

On the whole, Bayard Boudreau liked his job. It wasn't hard, and the pay was all right. Just about the only thing Bayard Boudreau did not like was getting up early. So when he telephoned Mr. Puttley to find out about that pickup the next morning and learned it was scheduled for seven-thirty a.m., he felt pretty grumpy about it.

Still, you didn't want to say no to Mr. Puttley, and you didn't want to be late, either, or anyway not so late that Mr. Puttley would hear about it. Bayard was staying at a Broad Street rooming house, not far from Cherry Street. He made a vow to himself to turn in early. But first, he'd pay just a quick visit to a local saloon he knew. A couple of drinks wouldn't hurt.

Chapter Fifty-Two

Caro awoke in a room that was pitch-dark and smelled like mothballs. She was enveloped in sheets and a blanket, but she was not in a bed. She seemed to be lying on cushions on the floor. And she was still wearing her clothes.

Gradually, the previous evening came back to her. Called into Mrs. George's office, confronted with her ink-stained shoes, Caro had admitted to having been in the apartment, but had refused to say anything else. It was strange, but the more Mrs. George had ranted and raved, the easier Caro had found it to be quiet. She never told about Jimmy or seeing the money in the freezer. As for explaining why she had gone to the apartment in the first place—well, she couldn't, could she?

How could anyone have explained about the mice and the newspaper story and the key?

When at last Mrs. George's energy flagged, Caro saw clearly what Jimmy had known all along. In spite of the photographs and the plaques and the letters from famous people, in spite of Caro's desperate need to believe in her, Mrs. George was a sham. Caro wasn't sure where the money in the freezer came from, but she thought it had something to do with Baby Charlie. Was it possible to sell a baby?

Caro had to think through a haze of drowsiness to reconstruct what had happened next. After Mrs. George had calmed down, she had offered cookies and tea, and Caro had said yes gratefully. She was thirsty and hadn't eaten dinner. The tea had lots of sugar in it, but even so it tasted bitter.

After that, Caro didn't remember anything.

Now, even in her muddled state, she understood what must have happened. There had been something in the tea, some kind of sleeping medicine.

Caro could see a line of light under the door to the cramped space where she lay. Could she be in the boss's apartment? And it was morning. But what time? Was the man still coming in the automobile to take her away? Where was she going?

Not to the well-off family with the two little sisters. That beautiful picture had been a lie.

Chapter Fifty-Three

When Mrs. George realized that Carolyn wouldn't tell her what she'd been doing in her apartment or what she had seen, she had left her momentarily in Polly's care and used Mrs. Spinelli's telephone to call Judge Mewhinney for advice. He, luckily, thought of the prescription powder he took to help him sleep and rushed over with two doses for Mrs. George to stir into Carolyn's tea.

Later, he had carried the sleeping child upstairs.

Now it was morning. Mrs. George rose early but waited till the last moment to awaken Carolyn. When she judged it was time, she opened the door of the walk-in closet, turned on the light, and knelt by the makeshift bed on the floor. Carolyn made a face but did not open her eyes. Mrs. George shook her shoulders.

"Carolyn? Dear, it's time to get up. The gentleman will be here in a moment to take you to your new family. Remember? Today's the day!"

"I know." Carolyn opened both eyes, and Mrs. George wondered if she'd been playing possum. "And I don't want to go."

"Nonsense, of course you do. You're just sad to leave your

friends. But I assure you you're going to be much happier with your own family."

Carolyn still didn't move. Mrs. George glanced at her watch: 7:25. Perhaps she shouldn't have waited so long to wake the girl. She didn't want Mr. Puttley's driver to be seen lurking around outside. There was no telling what type he might be.

"Carolyn dear, I must insist. On your feet now."

"Where am I? Why didn't I sleep in my own bed? Why am I still in my clothes?"

Dear heaven, could the child move more slowly? "I'll tell you everything when you're awake enough to hear it."

That worked. Carolyn sat up and rubbed her eyes. Mrs. George explained that she had been unwell the evening before, and so Mrs. George had decided to keep her upstairs in her own apartment as a precaution.

Did Carolyn believe her? How much did she remember? There was no way to know.

"I can't travel like this," Carolyn complained. "I'm all rumpled. My face isn't even washed."

"Yes, I know. My bathroom is here. There is a clean towel on the counter, and I've brought clean clothes up from your trunk."

When, a few minutes later, Carolyn emerged dressed, Mrs. George steered her out the door and down the stairs.

"Ma'am, where is my trunk? My suitcase? Will I be able to say good-bye to the others?"

The sleeping powder must have been potent, Mrs. George thought. Carolyn's speech was slightly slurred, and she was much more petulant than usual. On the whole, though, it was just as well if she wasn't thinking too clearly.

"The driver will take your trunk to the car for you," said Mrs. George. "And you already said your good-byes, don't you remember?"

"No," Carolyn said. "I don't."

Mrs. George didn't bother to contradict her. They were at the foot of the stairs now. Mrs. George's watch read 7:35. Mr. Puttley prided himself on the efficiency of his operations, so his man would be waiting. But when they stepped into the foyer, there was only Carolyn's trunk.

And whose voices were those she heard coming from the dining room? The exterminator was due shortly. The other children should have left for the park by now.

Could something have gone wrong?

Chapter Fifty-Four

Frank Kittaning had a cordial relationship with Helen George at the Cherry Street Children's Home...but he did not like her. The trouble was the disjunction between her personality and her job. She was cool, analytical, and authoritative, qualities that might have made her an excellent banker, business owner, or attorney. But instead, she ran a home for orphans, orphans she cared about primarily because they were the stock in trade of an orphanage.

Frank Kittaning liked children, and disliked the idea of a person indifferent to them being in charge. Still, he could find no fault with the Cherry Street Home, and in a job where he frequently saw children mistreated, this was a relief. The last thing an overworked child welfare inspector wanted was to make work for himself.

All of this is to say that Frank Kittaning was surprised when the switchboard rang through with a call from Helen George on a Saturday morning. By rights, he should not even have been at his desk. But he was working on the case of the baby's disappearance from the lying-in hospital, and a briefing with police was scheduled for later in the morning. He had wanted to take a look at the file first.

"This is Mrs. Helen George, headmistress of the Cherry Street Children's Home," said the voice on the telephone.

"Yes, of course, Mrs. George. What can I do for you?"

"I am calling about something important, Mr. Kittaning. A mighty important problem that we are having here. Can you come over right now?" Mr. Kittaning thought he heard whispering in the background. "It's a problem with an orphan, I mean."

Frank Kittaning rose from his chair, reached for his hat, and looked at his watch. "I can be there in ten minutes."

"Thank you. Okay. Good-bye," said Mrs. George, and the line went dead.

Mr. Kittaning's Packard was parked in the City Hall lot. He drove quickly, thinking that whatever the problem was, it must be serious. Mrs. George hadn't even sounded like herself.

Chapter Fifty-Five

Looking through the chipped marble portal that led to the foyer, Andrew took slow, even breaths and willed his heart to settle down. It was up to him to save the human pup that meant so much to Mary, and he would do it, too. Wasn't he the legendary art thief, the explorer of newsstands, the only rodent in all creation who had learned to read?

This assignment would be a piece of cake.

That's what he told himself. But he sure wished Mary were with him instead of sick with chills and fever in her nest.

Andrew had been terrified when he saw Mary become entrapped in the cold white box. That had never been part of the plan, and he had feared she wouldn't survive. The wait for the human pups to come upstairs, follow the ink tracks, and open the door to the box had been agonizing. Then, miraculously, his Mary had emerged unhurt, had returned to him safely.

Never in his eventful life had Andrew been so happy... until she had begun to sneeze and shiver. Andrew ordered her to bed, and she went obediently enough, but she would not let him nurse her. Instead, she insisted he continue to spy on the boss. Thus he learned about Caro's ink-stained shoes and subsequent confinement.

He had been reluctant to report this to Mary in her weakened state, but she insisted on hearing everything and suffered the consequences. If he didn't save Caro now, he feared the effect on Mary might be dangerous indeed.

So here he was with one final chance. He had all the confidence in the world that he was the mouse for the job. All he lacked was a plan.

Chapter Fifty-Six

Bayard Boudreau pulled up at the curb outside the Cherry Street Home at 8:05 a.m., only a few minutes—well, half an hour—late. He was unshaven and there were lead-colored bags beneath his bloodshot eyes. Worse yet, the stink of his breath was fierce, on account of his having eaten sausage and sauerkraut for supper the night before.

In the morning light, he would concede that he shouldn't've had that last glass at the bar. The sun was brighter than it had any right to be, and he had a splitting headache. *So help me,* he thought, *if that brat I'm driving today so much as speaks, I am going to clock her.*

A tall, white-haired biddy opened the home's heavy wooden door, and Bayard said good morning just as nice as you please.

"You're late" was all she said—little suspecting how lucky she was he didn't clock her, too, what with his headache and the sticky air and the bright sun and how hot it was. He hated summer. He hated daylight. He hated this evil old woman.

"I'll need some help with that trunk, ma'am," he told her.

"I'll find someone," she said. "Meanwhile, this is Carolyn." With her chin, she indicated a plain-looking girl who had something wrong with her right hand and arm. Burns, it looked like. She was frowning and pale. "Would you please help her out to the car? You can do that, can't you? Let's get this over with as expeditiously as possible...for the child's sake." The woman smiled a cottonmouth smile.

"Hustle her on outta here, that's what you're saying, ma'am?" Bayard said. "All right. I hope I know my job. Come on then, girly-girl. You're comin' with me. Car's waiting." He reached for the child's hand, but she stepped away. "Now, that's hurtful." He frowned and tried to look sad instead of angry.

"Go along with...uh...Mr. Puttley didn't give me your name, sir?"

"Boudreau."

"Go along with Mr. Boudreau."

"Who's Mr. Puttley?" The child took another step back.

Mr. Boudreau looked around him and noticed the marble, the chandeliers, the high ceilings. This was a nice place, quite a contrast to the conditions where the little girl was going. He could already see he didn't like her, not that there were any children he did like. He felt the weight of the gun in his jacket.

"Mr. Puttley is your new papa, dear," the old biddy said smoothly.

Bayard bit his lip to keep from laughing.

"I'm not going," the child said, and she planted her feet. "I don't like this man. Please...please, Mrs. George, don't make me go."

A flicker of something—sympathy?—crossed the woman's

face. For his part, Mr. Boudreau felt only irritation. He knew it was important that he not lose his temper. Mr. Puttley had warned him. But honestly, what was a guy supposed to do? Jesus Christ himself couldn't've stayed meek and mild when faced with an old witch and a stubborn little girl who kept you from getting your job done.

As it was, he'd have to drive all night. Mr. Puttley wouldn't like it if he was late.

With his last ounce of self-control, Mr. Boudreau spoke politely. "With your permission, ma'am. I have a schedule to which I must adhere." So saying, he encircled Carolyn with his arms, picked her up, and heaved her over his shoulder.

The old witch looked startled for a moment, then relieved. "It's for the best."

The little girl felt placid in his arms as he moved toward the door. He had been wrong about her. She wasn't going to give him any trouble. Maybe the witch had slipped her a Mickey Finn to slow her down.

The woman put her hand on the knob, turned it, and pushed open the door. Oh—the sunlight. Terrible! Mr. Boudreau felt a stab of pain at his temples and in the same instant something else. The girl transformed into a wildcat, kicking, scratching, and punching to get free at the same time she threw back her head and screamed—right into Bayard Boudreau's ear.

Chapter Fifty-Seven

Mr. Donald liked the kids at the Cherry Street Children's Home, even admired them, truth be told. Most were a darned sight more confident than he had been at their age. Growing up in a children's home himself, he had learned not confidence but obedience, a lesson reinforced by the United States Army.

Now his superior officer was Mrs. George and his standing order to make sure the Cherry Street kids did what they were supposed to. Usually, he was pretty good at it. The kids seemed to like him okay. He thought maybe in a couple of years he'd take advantage of the GI Bill, go to college, study to be a schoolteacher.

But this was the kind of morning that made a guy rethink his future. Matron Polly didn't feel well. Mrs. George was busy upstairs. In other words, Mr. Donald was flying solo...and wouldn't you know, something had gotten into these kids.

There had been Rice Krispies cereal for breakfast that morning, along with eggs and toast. The children had just been served when Jimmy and Melissa pushed back their chairs, stood up from the table, and walked out of the room. Did they so much as pause to ask permission? Not those two. And Mr. Donald couldn't very well follow them either. Who would have minded the others?

A short time later, the miscreants returned . . . but no number of demerits would induce them to say where they had been. When at last breakfast was over and the dishes cleared, Mr. Donald felt relieved. Fairmount Park would be just the thing for these characters. Let them run off their orneriness in the great outdoors.

"Line up two by two," he told them. "Our bus will meet us in the alley. We're going to leave through the kitchen and then the back door."

"Why are we going out the back door?" Virginia wanted to know.

"Where's Caro?" Betty asked.

"*Want Caro!*" Annabelle shouted.

So that was it, Mr. Donald thought. The kids were upset after all that business with Caro and her shoes last night. He didn't know where the girl was, either. The whole thing was mysterious. Mrs. Spinelli, like always, had a raft of dark theories, but none worth crediting.

"Something's going on out front," Jimmy said. "*Who's with me?*"

"Me!"

"Me!"

"All of us!"

The door between the dining room and the foyer was closed, but Jimmy raised his hand, and the children—by now an enthusiastic mob—advanced in his wake. Mr. Donald had lost control.

Chapter Fifty-Eight

First in dismay, then in panic, Mrs. George watched events unfold.

That fool of an unwashed driver dropped Carolyn to the floor, where she landed with a *thump*. Then, from behind, came children's voices, followed by a veritable herd blasting into the foyer, shouting and carrying on.

Hurrying after, ineffectual, came Mr. Donald.

"We want Caro! Where's Caro?"

What had come over her model orphans? This was too much to absorb all at once.

And Carolyn, sweet, responsible Carolyn, had become a screaming banshee! Mrs. George's well-controlled world was turning topsy-turvy at the worst possible moment.

Chapter Fifty-Nine

Caro had read the word *hysteria* in books but never understood it till now when she was fully in its grip—fighting the horrid smelly man who had dared to pick her up like a sack of vegetables. Then he dropped her, and she hit the floor—*Ow!*—and after that she heard Jimmy's voice shouting, then all the kids'.

The horrid smelly man, now in the doorway, shouted in fury over the din. "Shut up! For the love of Pete, would you all just—" And out of his jacket, he pulled something black and shiny—a gun.

For a moment, time stopped to accommodate this new reality. Then Annabelle burst into noisy tears, and Jimmy rushed forward as if fists were an adequate defense against bullets.

"Just you wait right—" Mr. Donald tried and failed to restrain Jimmy.

Meanwhile, from her vantage on the floor, Caro was the only one to see a soft gray form streaking toward Mr. Boudreau's unsuspecting shoe.

Chapter Sixty

Mrs. George saw Jimmy elude Mr. Donald's grasp and rush forward.

She saw Mr. Boudreau raise his gun. She saw the flash and heard the report, so loud it seemed to suck the air from the room as it echoed in her skull. For a moment, she thought she herself had been shot.

Then the ringing in her ears was replaced by renewed shrieking, wailing, and shouting. Someone was on the floor, someone else was caterwauling—having a fit.

This last was Mr. Boudreau, but what in the world asked him?

He was jumping, stomping his feet, and shrieking like a bee-stung two-year-old. *"Make it stop—get it away from me— help me-e-e!"*

At that moment, the front door opened and light flooded in. "My goodness—Mrs. George, what is going on?"

Frank Kittaning had arrived.

Mrs. George didn't stop to answer, didn't look back to learn the source of Mr. Boudreau's distress, didn't even look down to see who it was that lay on the floor with a bullet in him. Instead, she turned on her high heels and ran.

Chapter Sixty-One

It would be inaccurate to say that Mary Mouse was fighting for her life. In truth, she felt so miserable she had almost surrendered.

She knew she lay in a bed of fine sawdust and fresh, clean paper shreds in her own nest. She knew her paws had turned blue, but she wasn't sure why. She knew that Andrew had fussed over her incessantly, trying to make her comfortable. The tiny portion of her awareness that felt anything felt gratitude for this.

And where was Andrew now? A rescue mission, was that it? But Mary could not remember who it was that needed rescue.

Doesn't matter, Mary thought, letting sick misery overcome her, and with it visions like waking dreams. She saw her own dear mama and papa, long dead, and her youngest pups, Millie, Margaret, and Matilda. Were they dead, too? And if they weren't, why didn't they come to see her?

She saw her mate, Zelinsky. He was dead. She was sure of that. She remembered an argument they'd had and felt guilty all over again.

I've lost so much, she thought. *I guess it's time I join the dead myself.*

Then came a new vision, this one more solid than the others, a gangly shadow that blocked the light from the passageway. This vision—a large and somewhat unkempt male—seemed glad to see her but anxious, too.

Now she recognized him—Andrew Mouse, the legendary art thief, and he began to fuss, as was his way, annoying in his solicitude. Visions were never annoying, were they? Andrew must be real. He smelled real.

"Can I get you anything?" he asked. "Some dinner? At their breakfast, the children had that grain you like—the puffy one that crackles on the tongue. I could bring you some."

Returning to herself, Mary didn't care about food. "Caro?" she squeaked.

Andrew nodded. "Bit of a story to that, a good one. There I was, my dear, asking myself how to singlehandedly save the day. Then such a ruckus ensued! A giant noisome human! Rioting pups! Gunfire! Fortunately, I had a plan. It required split-second execution and utter disregard for my life and nostrils, but—"

Mary squeaked with the last of her strength. "Caro?"

"Ah," said Andrew. "Cut to the chase, you're saying. Well, here it is, then: She's been through a lot but no injuries sustained. I think she will be fine."

Mary felt a flood of relief, and with it new strength. She shifted, and when Andrew tried to prop up her head, she let him.

"Perhaps," she said, "I will have some dinner after all."

"*Ha ha ha ha ha!*" said Andrew. "I will be right back."

Chapter Sixty-Two

One good thing about being shot, you got an awful lot of sympathy...especially if you bled a lot, and Mr. Donald had. Something else good: You got to lie in bed while people brought you candy and flowers. Finally, once you got settled in at the hospital, you had plenty of time to think.

Mr. Donald had used that time to sort out all that had happened in those few minutes in the foyer at the Cherry Street Home...with one exception.

He didn't know what had startled the man who shot him—Bayard Boudreau, his name was. He had learned that later. Why had Bayard Boudreau missed? And why had he had a fit?

Jimmy had lunged at Mr. Boudreau to save Caro. Mr. Boudreau had produced a gun and aimed. Mr. Donald had reached for Jimmy, and Mr. Boudreau had fired.

But before Mr. Boudreau fired, something had caused him to jump and jerk the gun upward so that the bullet went over Jimmy's head and hit Mr. Donald in the shoulder. Down Mr. Donald had fallen, wondering if he was going to die...and thinking that would be ironic after he'd fought a war for three years without suffering a scratch.

Then, Mr. Donald remembered from the comfort of clean sheets in a peaceful, orphan-free room, Mr. Kittaning had arrived. Mr. Donald had always liked Mr. Kittaning, and from that moment his confidence had swelled. He was not going to die, and Mr. Boudreau was going to get his just deserts.

The hospital's visiting hours began at seven-thirty p.m. Mrs. Spinelli brought Jimmy by to see him.

"Hello, Donald." Mrs. Spinelli spoke very softly. "Are they treating you good?"

Donald tried to sit up to say they didn't have to speak in funeral voices, but pain shot through his shoulder and he gasped, convincing his visitors he ought to be treated with the reverence afforded someone who would soon reside with angels.

"I'm okay, yeah," Donald finally managed. "Is there any news?"

"You mean about the boss? Oh, boy, you'll never believe it," said Jimmy. "She got arrested! The policeman caught her trying to hotfoot it over the bridge to Camden in her automobile. They recognized the license plates after the description went out on the police radio. Mr. Kittaning explained it all to me."

"And that Mr. Boudreau fellow, he's been arrested as well," said Mrs. Spinelli.

"That's not any surprise, of course," said Jimmy. "He shot you!"

"Yes," said Mr. Donald.

"But he was trying to shoot me," said Jimmy.

"Yes," said Mr. Donald.

"What do you say to Mr. Donald, Jimmy?" Mrs. Spinelli nudged him with her elbow.

"Thank you," said Jimmy.

"There, that wasn't so hard, was it?"

Jimmy shrugged and twisted his face as if he was embarrassed.

"But what was Mr. Boudreau up to?" Donald asked. "Was he trying to kidnap Caro?"

"In a manner of speaking, he was," said Mrs. Spinelli. And she explained about Mr. Puttley, who kept kids like prisoners in a horrible place where they couldn't go to school and had to work like slaves. "Apparently, government authorities have tried to shut him down, but he paid off whoever he had to, and till now always stayed one step ahead."

Jimmy had nodded enthusiastically throughout Mrs. Spinelli's recitation. Now she paused and his words gushed forth. "With Mr. Boudreau trying to shoot me, they'll have enough to get Mr. Puttley, too, Mr. Kittaning says. Gosh, it's awful to think if Caro had ever had to go to a place like that. And Mrs. George was all ready to pack her off. They were in it together—her and Mr. Boudreau."

"But why did Mrs. George want to send Caro away?" Mr. Donald asked.

"Because Caro knew about the stolen babies!" said Jimmy.

"And so did I, only Mrs. George didn't know I knew. There was that baby Charlie she took for that movie star, and maybe other ones besides. If she'd known I knew, she would've been wanting to send me to work for Mr. Puttley, too!"

Mr. Donald thought Jimmy sounded wistful, as if he wanted some of Caro's drama for himself.

"How do they know she stole that baby?" asked Mr. Donald.

Jimmy and Mrs. Spinelli both tried to explain at once, with the result that the story took twice as long as it should have. In the end, Mr. Donald understood that the police had spoken to the baby's mother, and she had described the lady who took her baby away—a description that fit Mrs. George to a T. The baby himself had been located with Joanna Grahame, and she had agreed to return him to his rightful family.

"She was mostly wanting to make sure she got a full refund—that's the way she said it, according to Mr. Kittaning, 'a full refund,' and it was a pot of money, too. I never knew there was so much money in selling babies," said Jimmy.

"It sure was lucky Mr. Kittaning showed up when he did," said Mr. Donald.

Jimmy guffawed. "Lucky, my eye! That was my doing, mine and Melissa's. She telephoned him, pretending to be Mrs. George. Don't you remember when we left breakfast this morning? You were mad as a wet hen, but you couldn't do anything about it."

Mr. Donald remembered. "But I have one more question,"

he said. "I doubt you can answer it, though. What happened to Mr. Boudreau? He had you dead to rights, Jimmy, point-blank range…and then he missed. I would've asked about it at the time, but I was busy on the ground writing in agony and bleeding to death."

Mrs. Spinelli shrugged. She didn't know. As for Jimmy, he had his suspicions, but chose not to speak them out loud.

Chapter Sixty-Three

With Jimmy's help, the police recovered the money, birth certificates, and other records from Mrs. George's hiding place in the freezer. Based on that evidence—and testimony from Judge Mewhinney and Matron Polly—Mrs. George was convicted of kidnapping racketeering and child endangerment and sent to prison for life. In exchange for their testimony, Polly and the judge earned leniency from the court, but Judge Mewhinney would be looking for a new line of work. He had lost his license to practice law.

Initially, the newspapers had been all over the Cherry Street scandal, but with a few well-placed invitations, Mr. and Mrs. Philips-Bodbetter were able to demonstrate to publishers that the orphans themselves had never ceased to thrive, thus preserving the institution's reputation. Soon they also found a new director and a new girls' matron. Mrs. Spinelli, having had nothing to do with selling babies, stayed on. So did Mr. Donald, who at the same time announced his intention of enrolling in college the following fall.

For most of the children, the changes at the home didn't make much difference. The new director had a gentler manner than Mrs. George, and the new matron was stricter than

Matron Polly. But the lessons, comforts, and chores went on as before, and these—along with the friendships among the children—were what mattered day to day.

It was different for Caro. Mrs. George's disgrace had upended her world. She had admired Mrs. George, wanted to be equally elegant, refined, and self-possessed. Now she knew she had admired a monster, and that made her feel like one herself—compromised, low, and unworthy.

And, she told herself as she lay in bed sleepless night after night, she shouldn't have been surprised. She had shown her true self when she abandoned her mother the night of the fire. So of course she hadn't stood up to Mrs. George the way Jimmy had. She had been a selfish coward, protecting her place as Mrs. George's favorite.

One day in late September, the new director asked to see Carolyn in her office. Mrs. Burnett had had the walls repainted. Mrs. George's plaques and testimonials had been replaced with watercolor paintings of children and flowers. But the furniture was the same, and Caro felt uncomfortable sitting where she had sat so many times before.

"Everyone is worried about you, Caro," said Mrs. Burnett, "and one person in particular."

"I'm fine, thank you, ma'am," Caro said. "I can talk to Jimmy myself if you want."

"It wasn't Jimmy I meant, although he is a fine boy. It's

Mr. Frank Kittaning. You know he has always taken a special interest in you."

"Mr. Kittaning is very kind," Caro said without much interest in him or his concern for her. One thing about not eating and not sleeping, you cease to be very interested in anything.

"In fact," Mrs. Burnett continued, "Mr. Kittaning would like to take you out for ice cream if that's all right with you."

Caro might be feeling terrible, but she wasn't so far gone that she didn't want ice cream. "I don't mind."

Mrs. Burnett smiled. "All right, that's lovely. I'll tell him and perhaps we can set things up for tomorrow."

The soda fountain was on Walnut Street. Caro didn't want to be greedy, so she ordered a single scoop of vanilla.

Frank Kittaning frowned. "Caro? You can do better than that. My own daughter's younger than you, and she likes strawberry ice cream sodas. Do you like strawberry ice cream sodas?"

"I think so," Caro said. She had never had one. It sounded fancy.

"I'll join you, then," said Mr. Kittaning, and he ordered two. When they came, they were in tall goblets with cherries on top.

With its gold chairs and white tables, the soda fountain was the loveliest place Caro had ever been, and in spite of herself, she felt better. Mr. Kittaning was kind. The pink soda was delicious. It was a sunny day, and the other people in the soda shop were smiling and laughing. They didn't know she was wicked. They probably thought she was as good as anyone else.

"Caro, what did Mrs. George tell you about the day of the accident, the fire?" Mr. Kittaning asked after a while.

Caro's pleasure evaporated, and she wanted to say "Nothing" or "I don't want to talk about it." Instead, some instinct—or possibly just the good influence of ice cream— told her to trust him.

"She told me I ran away," Caro said, "and left my mama to die. She told me I was a coward, but it was okay because a lot of people are cowards. She told me if I was very good, then God might be able to forgive me. So I tried to be good. I really, really tried."

On those last words her voice broke, and she closed her eyes to squeeze back the tears. What, she wondered, did those happy, laughing people think of her now? She was determined not to put on a show. So she took a few ragged breaths and wiped away the lone tear that had escaped. When she opened her eyes, she saw the expression on Mr. Kittaning's face and asked, "Are you okay?"

He nodded, took a breath, let it out, and spoke very softly. "Oh, Caro, no. That's not what happened at all. And of all the horrible lies Mrs. George told to so many people, I think maybe that was the worst."

"What do you mean?"

"You didn't run away, Caro. You ran to help your mother, but it was already too late. The firemen had to pry you away. You were pounding on the door, trying to turn the knob— that's how you were burned. By then, you had inhaled so much smoke, you were near to passing out. Even so, when they picked you up to carry you to safety, you kicked and struggled, trying to go back."

Caro didn't believe him. "How would you even know?"

"Because I was there, Caro. I wrote the report, interviewed the firemen. All along, I thought you knew the true story. That's why I never said anything. You were only six years old, but you were a fighter."

Caro finished her soda, aware only that Mr. Kittaning was a nice man and the day was sunny and she had just learned she liked strawberry ice cream sodas. Her gloom had begun to dissipate, but as yet she didn't know it.

Chapter Sixty-Four

During the upheaval in human territory, Mary and Andrew lay low, keeping an eye on Caro, glad when at last they heard her laugh again.

"Do you think she knows what she owes us?" Andrew asked Mary over breakfast one evening in October.

"You're the one who tackled the shoe of that singularly nasty human, slipped beneath his trouser cuff, and ran up his leg." Picturing this made Mary shiver with disgust. "For that, she may indeed owe you. But I owe her my life."

Later that night, the two mice at last got around to hanging a new picture in their nest. It was the one they had found in the box with the gray metal key on the boss's desk. How the picture got into the box neither of them knew, but they were art thieves, so they took it.

This picture was not a portrait. Rather, it depicted a full-grown male human alongside a large and mysterious animal pulling a vehicle with enormous wheels. The words said: *Minnesota Territorial Centennial 1849–1949. Red River Ox Cart.*

The picture was just the kind of window to a world beyond the colony that Mary liked to ponder. Was the Minnesota territory nearby? What were the mice like there? And the ani-

mal in the picture—was it called an ox? It was bigger than the human but seemed to be obeying him. Or maybe the cart belonged to the ox, and it was the human that obeyed.

The following day, Andrew was giving Mary a reading lesson near the alley door when a scout entered through the portal there. His name, he said, was Tobias. He was young and very nervous.

"Ex-ex-excuse me, Auntie, uh…Uncle? Chief Director Randolph sent me," he stammered.

After such a long time, it was a shock to hear another mouse voice and see another mouse frame. And what did this young one want?

Andrew sat back on his haunches and fluffed his fur. "What is your mission, Tobias?" he asked.

"To establish whether it's safe for the colony to return, sir. Uh...excuse, me, Uncle, uh...are you Andrew Mouse? If you don't mind my asking? I grew up on stories about Andrew Mouse. Is that you?"

"*Ha ha ha ha ha!*" said Andrew. "Yes, as a matter of fact. Do any particular stories come to mind?"

Mary interrupted. "My pups," she said, "Millie, Margaret, and Matilda Mouse. Do you have news of them?"

Flustered, the scout looked from Andrew to Mary. "Apologies, Auntie. I should have reported. They are well. They send their love."

Mary felt weak with relief and overjoyed at the possibility she might yet see her darlings again. Even after all that had happened, she had never lost hope.

"Why did the chief director send you?" Andrew asked. "Are conditions poor where you are living?"

They were, it turned out. The humans in the new home were very tidy, never left crumbs, set traps every night. Some of the young mice had been caught, and there was precious little to eat. The mice were facing a cold and hungry season.

"Our spies report there is a new boss at the Cherry Street Home," said Tobias. "Are there any residual toxins from the extermination?"

Andrew fixed the scout with a gimlet eye. "Do we look as if we'd been exterminated?"

Tobias opened and closed his jaws; Mary suppressed a laugh. "No exterminator came," she explained. "It was a lot of brouhaha over nothing."

"In fact, this territory remains quite a nice one," Andrew assured him. "The predator is also gone. New management has allergies."

Tobias dipped his nose and flipped his tail. "I must be off to file my report."

"Scurry safe," they told him…and only days thereafter, the Cherry Street colony returned.

This time the migration came off with minimal casualties and only a single fatality, Chief Director Randolph himself, who fell behind his division and was ambushed by a rat. In due course, a state funeral was conducted with all the pomp and ceremony traditionally accorded a great leader.

Pleading headaches, neither Mary nor Andrew attended.

Mary's reunion with her pups was happiness itself. And when Millie, Margaret, and Matilda found out that Andrew had taught their mother to read—well, they wouldn't stop squeaking till he agreed to teach them.

"You don't think the other pups will want to learn, do you?" Andrew asked Mary.

"Oh, yes," she assured him. "The pups, the auditors— every mouse will want to learn."

Andrew remembered Stuart Little's experience teaching school and sighed. "I fear my new job will be harder than the old one."

Chapter Sixty-Five

———◆◇◆———

Caro wasn't convinced at first that Mr. Kittaning had told the true story about the fire. Still, she started sleeping better, and her appetite came back. Then, after a few days, she saw in her mind's eye something long forgotten: a pattern of tiny green leaves on a white background, the wallpaper in the hallway between her bedroom and her mother's.

Along with the image came powerful sensory memories that included the sound of her own voice screaming *"Mama!"* and the pain in her throat and chest that silenced her screams at last.

In their house, Caro's bedroom had been near the front, while her mother's adjoined the kitchen in the rear. If Caro had run away that night, she would never have been in that hallway at all. Nothing would bring back her mother. But from that moment, Caro began to rebuild her sense of herself based on a new story, a true story. And unlike the story Mrs. George had told, this one gave her strength.

Soon the other intermediates registered Caro's improved spirits and felt free to press their one remaining question: How had she and Jimmy known to look in Mrs. George's freezer? Caro tried evasion, then hit upon a better idea, the truth: "The mice that live in the walls told us."

This provoked stunned silence, a collective *"Ewww,"* and more questions: "How did the mice find out?" "How many are there?" "How do they live?"

Caro's knowledge of the mice was more limited than her listeners' curiosity. To satisfy them, she invented a world within the walls. And the more she told her friends about it, the more they wanted to know. It was a pleasure for them to imagine their home from the perspective of creatures even smaller than children and more modest than orphans.

On a Friday morning in November, the students in Miss Ragone's class were restless. It may have been sunspots or barometric pressure or possibly the new brand of cereal, Sugar Crisp, that Mrs. Spinelli had served at breakfast. Whatever it was, spelling went nowhere, and neither did long division or world capitals.

At her wits' end, Miss Ragone pulled out her secret weapon, a book.

"Where were we?" she asked the suddenly attentive children.

"Mr. Toad just crashed the caravan," Jimmy answered.

Miss Ragone found the place and began to read but had completed only a paragraph when Virginia interrupted. "Read louder, Miss Ragone, so the mice can listen, too!"

Miss Ragone repeated, "Mice?"

"They live in the walls," Barbara explained.

"They have churches and grocers and saloons," said Bert.

"Oh, dear," said Miss Ragone.

"They drink root beer," said Jimmy.

"And they have tiny bicycles and tiny Victrolas," said Barbara.

"And how do you know all this?" Miss Ragone asked.

The children glanced at one another but, for the first time that morning, were silent. At last, Caro spoke up. "I told them."

"Did you, Carolyn?" said Miss Ragone. "And are these stories of yours true?"

Caro looked over at Jimmy, who was trying not to laugh. "They're true," she said, "but not entirely factual."

Miss Ragone smiled. "I see. Well, in that case, I will raise my voice a little."

Miss Ragone read two chapters before lunch. Then all the children except one erupted from their desks and jostled their way out of the room.

In the doorway, Miss Ragone looked back and asked, "Are you coming, Carolyn?"

Still caught up in the story, Caro dawdled. "Yes, ma'am. Jimmy will save me a seat."

Caro finished straightening her papers and put her pencils in their box before standing up and starting for the door. On her way, she spotted something tiny, soft, and gray at the base of the back wall of the classroom—a mouse sitting up on its haunches, paws folded neatly over its heart. The paws weren't blue anymore. Even so, Caro recognized her friend's pure white whiskers and air of perfect calm.

"Mousie, how are you? Climb up now so we can talk. We don't have long. Miss Ragone usually eats at her desk." Caro knelt and extended her palm. The mouse stepped aboard. "Were you listening to the stuff about the mice in the walls? Now, don't you worry. The other kids think it's like a fairy tale, and Jimmy and I—we'll never say different."

For a moment, mouse and human regarded one another with all the kindness, goodwill, and curiosity available to their respective species. Neither would ever understand the other. Each believed it was worthwhile to try.

Caro started to thank her friend for everything, but when the mouse cocked its pink half-moon ear, Caro stopped to listen, too. Miss Ragone was coming back. Hastily, the girl knelt, released her friend, and raised her pinkie finger to wave. To her surprise, the mouse raised its paw in return. "Oh!" Caro gasped, delighted, and at the same moment Miss Ragone came in, carrying a lunch tray.

"Carolyn, dear," she said, "what are you doing down there? Are you all right?"

Caro stood up and turned to face her teacher. "I'm fine, Miss Ragone. I was just saying good-bye to a friend."

Miss Ragone frowned. "Indeed? And was it . . . one of your mice?"

"Yes," said Caro.

Miss Ragone set down her lunch tray and spoke gently. "Carolyn, you know, don't you, that real mice are dirty and make all kinds of mischief? They're vermin is what they are, nothing like the ones in the stories you tell."

Caro nodded. "Don't worry, Miss Ragone. I'm not crazy. I like to tell stories, is all."

Miss Ragone looked relieved. "I'm glad to hear it. Now hurry down to lunch, dear. It's macaroni and cheese today."

Caro grinned. "Hooray—the mice love macaroni and cheese." Then she dashed out the door before Miss Ragone could reply.